NOV 18 2004	DATE DUE	
DEC 4 2004		
JAN 10 2005		
JAN 19 2005		
FEB 9 2005		

THE LITTLE WHITE CAR

THE LITTLE WHITE CAR

a novel

Danuta de Rhodes

CANONGATE U.S.
New York

First published in the UK in 2004 by
Canongate Books Ltd., Edinburgh, Scotland

Printed in the United States of America

FIRST AMERICAN EDITION

ISBN 1-84195-589-2

Canongate U.S.
841 Broadway
New York, NY 10003

04 05 06 07 08   10 9 8 7 6 5 4 3 2 1

Many thanks to La Ginge, Léonie 'Smot' Tancred and Stan Stanton for their invaluable reading skills, my naked landlady Christel Manbique, Tama Janowitz and family and ferrets for the cold soup in a can, 'Drivetime' James Mansbridge, Gina Garan, Colin McLear, Nguyen Thi Quynh Thanh, Peter Finlay, Blythe, the literary hostess Jenita Colganova, Jamie Byng and everybody else at Canongate for everything (all of which is good), all my other publishers around the world, everyone who said I shouldn't quit, Mae Emmily Magtalas, the de Rhodes family and all my friends in high and low places – Danuta loves you all.

PART ONE

CHAPTER ONE

One of the things about The Sofia Experimental Breadboard Octet was that they weren't an octet. There were fourteen of them. Another thing about them was that none of the fourteen played a breadboard. There were two drummers, one who played with brushes and another who played with the backs of his hands, a left-handed flautist, a woman who, despite being classically trained, played the clarinet with only three fingers, a vibraphonist who sometimes moved over to the saw, and various people drifting between all sorts of other instruments, tools, tape machines and kitchen equipment, none of which was a breadboard. The Sofia Experimental Breadboard Octet were, however, experimental. They were also from Sofia. That is to say they were based in Sofia. In fact two of the octet, identical twin sisters, were from Bucharest, another was from Berlin, and the rest were from various parts of Bulgaria, but all fourteen had called Sofia their home since the early nineties, and the line up had never changed.

Jean-Pierre slowly explained all this to his girl-friend, Veronique, as he took their third album, *Where Soundwaves Turn To Sound*, out of its case and put it into the CD drawer of his small and expensive stereo.

She took a long drink of white wine and said, 'Oh.'

'It's not really songs,' he said. 'It's more like soundscapes.'

She took another long drink of wine, and said, 'Ah.'

'Listen,' he said, pressing play on the remote control and settling back, stretching out on the floor with his head resting against the armchair.

The Sofia Experimental Breadboard Octet delib-erately started their first track two minutes and fifteen seconds into the CD, as if to make their listeners wonder whether they were missing something inaudible yet sonically extraordinary. During the silence Veronique took some of her hair in her fingers, separated three strands and started to turn them into a plait. It was a habit she had picked up when she had had long hair, and she still did it even though her hair was now cut too short for her to be able to make a plait of any significance.

'You're not concentrating,' said Jean-Pierre.

She didn't say anything, but she stopped plaiting her hair. It wasn't something she felt strongly enough about for it to be the cause of an argument. She tried concentrating on the silence instead, and eventually the music began. A third of her half-listened to it, another third of her thought about other things, and the other third just looked around the room that had become so familiar over the eight months she had spent as a regular visitor to Jean-Pierre's apartment, at the almost bare walls in the dim light of the carefully placed lamps and candles, and at the floor and the doors.

She was sitting at the far end of the sofa, out

of the way of Jean-Pierre's outstretched legs. He was wearing his old leather boots. She didn't know why. She hadn't been paying the closest attention, but she was fairly sure he hadn't been wearing them when they had made love earlier in the evening, and since they weren't going to be going anywhere, as usual, she didn't see the point of him putting them on. She supposed it was just one of those stupid, annoying things he did. He was also wearing thick woolen socks. It was still August, just, and it was easily warm enough for him to go around without hiking socks on his feet.

He had, as usual, rolled six fat joints before she had arrived, and laid them in line on a plate. He had smoked three already, offering each one to her. She had declined every time. He lit the fourth, slowly rolling his head around as he held the smoke in his lungs, and then exhaling with his lips curled in a way that had lost him friends. People who had been undecided about whether or not they liked him had backed off after seeing this display, as he closed his eyes with such exaggerated indifference as the smoke blew slowly from a perfect hole on the right hand side of his mouth and hung in the air like seraphim. 'He's in love with himself,' they would say to each other afterwards. 'Did you see what he did with his smoke?' Veronique had heard this quite a few times.

She refilled her glass, and he offered her the joint. She had told herself that, for once, she was going to spend an evening at Jean-Pierre's place without getting stoned. She had been doing very well, but there was something about *Where Soundwaves Turn To Sound* by The Sofia Experimental Breadboard Octet that made her feel she had no choice, so she reached over and took it. She smoked it for a while, then handed it back.

After eighteen minutes the first track ended. Usually he would press pause on the remote control between pieces of music, and deliver a short lecture about what they had just heard, but this time he just looked at the ceiling instead, letting the CD play on. He blinked, very slowly.

The joint had gone out in the ash tray. She relit it, and held on to it for a while before passing it back to him and going back to her wine. Track two seemed to be the same as track one, the only difference being that it was a lot shorter. It ended after less than a minute. Jean-Pierre picked up the remote control, pointed it at the stereo and paused the CD.

'I've got to get them over here,' he said.

She had heard this kind of talk many times before. He often spoke at great length about how he was going to arrange a series of unique avant-garde music evenings in spectacular venues. They would be packed with appreciative people and given rave reviews, and their reputation would build with such momentum that each one would sell out weeks in advance. They would make him money, enable him to evangelise about the music he loved, and turn him into the celebrated Bohemian he had always wanted to be. He would be respected throughout Paris and across the world by musicians he admired, and his name would be known by people who mattered to him.

In the early days of their relationship Veronique had thought that he really was on the verge of becoming somebody interesting, but as months went by without anything happening she realised that he would never really come close to arranging a concert, or starting a record label, or getting his own band together. She knew that at some point over the coming month or two he would make a call to someone or other about the logistics of attaining work permits for fourteen Sofia-based avant-garde musicians, and find out that it would be a lengthy process involving the filling in of lots of forms. He would ask her to help out. She would say no, that she was too busy doing her own things, and that anyway they were only forms and not such a big deal, and he would abandon his plans, citing her lack of support as the main reason, maybe even the only reason, for the project's failure.

'What do you think?' he asked.

Veronique turned down the corners of her mouth, and shrugged.

He pressed pause, and track three began. She finished her wine and refilled her glass. She yawned. The bottle, their second of the evening, was nearly empty, and Jean-Pierre had only had about one and a half glasses all night. She hadn't meant to drink nearly so much, but there hadn't been a lot else to do. She felt her eyelids grow heavy. Jean-Pierre stubbed out the remains of the joint and lay back on the floor, his eyes closed.

After a while Veronique heard something in the music that she recognised. She couldn't quite place it. It went away, so she stopped thinking about it. She went back to her wine, and to looking at the wall. The music carried on, with no apparent tune or form. Then it happened again. Somewhere within the murk of track three was a tune that she recognised.

She hummed in her head. A few bars later the notes came around again. 'Yes,' she said, coming to life and raising her glass to toast her discovery. 'I've got it.'

Jean-Pierre looked at her without smiling. He leaned forward and lit the fifth joint. Then he settled back down and closed his eyes.

'Listen,' Veronique said.

It took a while for the familiar part of the tune to come around again, but when it did she sang along.

He looked at her with disgust.

'No, really,' she said. 'Wait.'

The tune sank back into the drone of the soundscape, but when it returned she sang along once again. 'Can't you hear it?'

'No,' he said. 'I can't hear it at all.' But he was lying. It was with horror that he realised that The Sofia Experimental Breadboard Octet had included the tune of the chorus of Vanessa Paradis's 'Joe Le Taxi' as a recurring flourish in track three of *Where Soundwaves Turn To Sound*. It was slower than the original, and probably played on a trombone, but the notes were exactly the same as the vocal melody. 'You don't know what you're talking about,' he said. He shivered, hoping that it was a coincidence on the octet's part, that they wouldn't cite early Paradis as a primary influence alongside Karlheinz Stockhausen, John Coltrane and Holger Czukay. He started to wonder whether arranging a concert for them would be such a good idea after all.

The tune came around again, and Veronique jumped to her feet. She stepped into her shoes and started singing along, and dancing just like Vanessa Paradis in the video.

'There is no connection,' said Jean-Pierre.

Veronique carried on dancing.

'You should stop that now,' he said.

'No way.'

'You are tone deaf.'

She hadn't thought about 'Joe Le Taxi' for a long time, but she still loved it. She hadn't always been ready to admit that she loved it, but she always had. It reminded her of times spent having fun.

'You know nothing about music,' said Jean-Pierre. 'You've never played a note of it in your life, every record you own is bad, and you don't appreciate the musical education I give you. You just don't begin to understand it.'

She ignored him. 'People used to say I looked like Vanessa Paradis,' she said.

'Horseshit,' he snapped, sitting up. His eyes were even more hooded than usual. 'That is total fucking horseshit.'

'So you don't think I'm pretty enough?' The tune came around again, and Veronique sang along.

'You have completely the wrong shape head.'

'What? In a good way or a bad way?'

'What do you mean?'

'I mean if my head's the wrong shape in a bad way why didn't you tell me a long time ago? I would have changed the shape of my head for you.'

'I'm not saying it's the wrong shape in a bad way, it's just different from Paradis's head. She has a very distinctive head shape, as you know.'

'And you prefer her head to mine. I see.'

'I'm not going to argue about whose head I prefer, but you don't look anything like her.'

'Well, people said I did. When this song came out . . .'

'This is not "Joe Le-fucking-Taxi",' he snapped. 'This is track three of *Where Soundwaves Turn To Sound* by The Sofia Experimental Breadboard Octet. It doesn't have a name. It doesn't need one.'

'OK, when "Joe Le Taxi" came out I must have been about . . .' she squinted at the ceiling in concentration, '. . . let me think . . . When did it come out?'

'I don't fucking know. I don't fucking care.'

She thought for a moment longer, then said, 'I'm twenty-two now, and it's 1997. It must have been around 1987, when I was twelve, because that was when my grandmother died and I went to stay with my cousin Valerie from Lille who is my age, well, six weeks younger, and we watched the video over and over again and we learned the dance. Look.' She moved from side to side with a studied listlessness. 'And when my aunt asked us what we would like to cheer us up we asked to go shopping for clothes and we both picked outfits like ones we'd seen Vanessa wearing on TV. They weren't . . .' She tilted her head to one side, bit her lip and raised the index finger of her right hand. 'Here it comes . . .'

Again she sang and danced along. Jean-Pierre looked at the floor and shook his head. When the tune vanished back into the formless soundscape she stopped singing but carried on dancing from side to side, as though there were a rhythm to follow.

'. . . they weren't exactly like the outfits on TV,

but they were as close as we could get from the shops in Lille. And we had to wear our old shoes because my aunt wouldn't buy us new ones, and that made us mad. That was when people started saying I looked like her, even though the clothes weren't quite right, and my hair is dark brown, almost black, and I've got completely the wrong shape head. But they still said I looked like her.'

'Which you don't,' he said. His head was in his hands.

'But look at my eyes. They aren't so different from hers – they're pretty much the same colour, at least. And look at this.' She raised her top lip, and pointed. 'I've got a gap between my front teeth. It's nowhere near as wide as the gap she has between *her* front teeth, I know, but it's still a gap, and my hair came down to here in those days,' she drew a line with her finger a few centimetres above her left elbow, 'it wasn't short like it is now. And I would do this . . .' She stuck her lips out a bit. 'I used to do that all the time. I wanted to be her more than anything in the world.'

Track three ended. There was a pause, then track four began.

She sat down. Now the music had changed to what sounded like the slowed down creak of a rusty car door she felt sleepy again, and miserable. She wanted to talk to somebody about whether or not she should grow her hair again, or about how most of the people who had told her she looked like Vanessa Paradis had been middle-aged men who wouldn't usually have been able to tell one pop star from the next. She hadn't realised at the time what had really been going through their minds as they complimented her on her likeness. But Jean-Pierre wouldn't want to talk about things like that. He preferred to talk about things like 'harmonics', and 'cadence', whatever they were. He passed her the joint. It didn't make things any better. She looked at him. His dark brown hair hung over his shoulders. It was probably the same as it had always been, but lately it had seemed lifeless and boring. The way he nodded along to the erratic flow of the music annoyed her.

'You know,' she said, 'Jesus was dead by the time he was your age.'

She had baked Jean-Pierre a cake on his birthday, and had spelled out the number thirty-four in thirty-four candles.

'What do you care about Jesus?'

She started back on the wine. It didn't make him any younger, and it didn't make her look any more or less like Vanessa Paradis. She thought for a while about coming on to him, covering his face with smoky kisses and letting him run his hands under her dress, but the thought bored her. It seemed so old. She stood up.

'I'm going now,' she said.

He looked at her.

'Can I have that?' she asked, pointing at the last of Jean-Pierre's joints. He passed it to her, and she put it in her bag. 'Thank you,' she said.

'Are you really going?' he asked. She had never left before, at least not until the morning.

She didn't say anything. She just put her brown suede jacket on. She had bought it the week before, and he hadn't said a word about it, as though it

17

were just *her jacket*, the one she always wore, and not something new, and fashionable, and a lot more expensive than she could really afford.

'I'll call you tomorrow,' he said.

'No. Don't call me tomorrow. Don't call me at all.' She had been thinking about saying that for a while. She was pleased with the way it sounded.

He said nothing.

She called César, her Saint Bernard who had been dozing on a big cushion in the corner of the room, and put him on his lead. She looked at Jean-Pierre. She hadn't expected him to look so sad. Her camera was in her bag and she thought about taking a photograph of him, lying on the floor – she would call it 'Wounded Man', or something like that. But she didn't. It somehow wouldn't seem right, and anyway it would have been too much effort for the state she was in.

'Come on César,' she said, leading her dog towards the door as the music, if you could call it that, droned on. Jean-Pierre looked at the floor-boards, or the rug. She couldn't tell which.

CHAPTER TWO

She walked along the street to her car. The back seat was down to make room for César, and he clambered up and lay down. She got in, shut the door and fumbled for the cigarette lighter. Her parents had bought the old Fiat in Normandy the week before, after their Renault had finally died during a holiday at the apartment they shared with various relatives, and it was the first time she had smoked in it. It took her a while to find the small black button in the dark. When it popped out she lit the joint and sat behind the wheel, knowing she was in no state to drive home.

'I've left him, César,' she said.

It was after midnight and she was tired, so she

decided to sleep right there. The sunlight would wake her up before Jean-Pierre left the house, so he wouldn't see her spending the night in her car with her Saint Bernard asleep in the back. She reclined her seat as far as it would go, and looked at the soft light coming from Jean-Pierre's window. She remembered how impressed she had been eight months before when, after meeting him at a party, she had gone back there and seen his shelves lined with CDs by people she had never heard of, and books by writers whose names she knew but who she had never read – people like Hubert Selby Jr., Henry Miller, Kerouac, Bukowski and Julio Cortázar, whose *Hopscotch* she later found was Jean-Pierre's bible. Sometimes he cursed himself for having been born in Paris, wishing he could have come to the city from South America like Horacio Oliveira, the star of the book. He was sure that having been born there was in some way holding him back. One drunken evening he had told her how he often passed the spot near his old primary school where he had tripped over a brick, grazed his knee and put his hand in a pile of dog's mess. It would feel as if the last twenty five years had never happened – he could still smell the shit and hear the taunts of the other children. He asked her how he could be expected to enjoy going to see the fish on the Quai de la Mégisserie knowing that at any moment a friend of his mother could walk by and recognise him, and stop to ask him how he is, and whether he's still playing his gigantic saxophone, and whether or not he has a proper job yet, even though they can tell just by looking at him that he hasn't. He would see in their eyes the pity they felt for his mother to have ended up with a son like that, one who hasn't grown up and who looks as though he never will. If he had spent his early years in Argentina he would have been free to walk the streets of Paris as if the past had never happened.

Among his books was a cluster by Anaïs Nin, six in a row. Veronique knew that a load of semi-intellectual books and records was nothing much to be impressed by, and, thinking about it, it struck her that she had only really been impressed back then because it had suited the moment for her to be the wide-eyed girl. He was, after all, the oldest man she had ever been with. But the Anaïs Nin books stood out from the others, and she had concluded that if he was an avid reader of hers then he must also be a master of the erotic arts, profoundly aware of the desires of women, and she wanted to find out what he knew. He put on a CD of some slow, dissonant music that she didn't recognise, and didn't think much of, and before long he was licking her ear and sliding his hand across her belly and down the back of her jeans. She had no way of knowing that his last girlfriend had moved out two weeks before, after a short and awful cohabitation, and had taken everything of hers except an ugly pepper mill, a pair of green gloves with a hole in the left thumb, a half-empty tub of taramasalata and those six books by Anaïs Nin.

She hadn't been sure what Anaïs Nin would have made of his almost silent lovemaking, of the way he spent so long on her breasts, or the way he smoked three cigarettes while spending about half an hour inside her, reaching out to the bedside table and using only his right hand to take each cigarette from the packet, bring it to his lips, light it, flick the ash over the side of the bed and, when each one was finished, to reach down and stub it out on the floorboards. He never once broke his rhythm, dropped ash on her or blew smoke in her eyes. Maybe Anaïs Nin would have thought he was handsome enough to get away with it, and been pleased that his hair tickled her shoulders, and noticed that his penis was a bit thicker than the others she had encountered, as if it had grown with age like a tree trunk. Maybe she would have daydreamed happily through the monotonous bits, and maybe, when he finished and dropped the soggy condom on to the floor, and mumbled, *That was good*, Anaïs Nin would have kissed him too, and said, *Yes, it was good*, and thought, *This isn't just a one night thing – I have a new boyfriend now.*

But that had been all there was, Veronique thought as she tried to make herself comfortable in the driver's seat. More or less everything they experienced together they experienced that first night. Since then it had been like watching the same film over and over again. A film that was good, in some ways very good, but which never stopped being the same, no matter how many times you watched it.

A man walked past the car, and she watched

him disappear around a dark corner. She carried on smoking, and thinking about Jean-Pierre, and César, and her camera, and her boring job. Another man appeared from around the same corner, and walked towards her. She began to wonder if he was in fact the same man, coming back to have another look at her, and she made sure the doors were locked.

'Look after me César,' she said.

The man walked quickly past the car, and, just for a moment, his eyes met hers. She put her key into the ignition, put on her seatbelt and turned the engine over. She decided to go back home. There was no way she could feel safe there with that man walking past her all the time, even if he was really two men and they were the nicest men in France – men who spent their Saturdays dressed as grapes, standing in busy streets and rattling tins for unhappy children. And despite her beautiful brown jacket it would probably become too cold to sleep in the car, even if she was to huddle in the back with César. Anyway the night air and the fear had seemed to sober her up.

Slowly and carefully she drove away, not missing Jean-Pierre for a moment.

CHAPTER THREE

She turned on the radio. A man was talking very softly about the weather in the Dordogne. As she tried to work out which buttons she would have to press to move from station to station the car began to drift on to the wrong side of the road, but there didn't seem to be anybody around to notice and she pulled it back on course as soon as she realised.

She started to think about the things she could do now she had got rid of him. 'I'm only twenty two,' she said to César, craning her neck to find him in the rear view mirror, 'but I've been living like an old woman.' She supposed that even Jeanne Calment, who had died earlier that month at the age of a hundred and twenty two, a whole century ahead of her, must have had better times that year. She had seen the old woman's nursing home in Arles on television, and it had seemed like the glory days of the Moulin Rouge compared to Jean-Pierre's apartment.

Dancing to the tune of 'Joe Le Taxi' had made her think of her friend Estelle, and she tried to remember the last time they had been out together. It had been ages, more like months than weeks. They had been friends since school. Estelle had always been ahead of Veronique and their other friends when it came to knowing how to go about her business. She was the first to get herself a real boyfriend – a sullen character with a horribly pale face and lots of wild hair, who ravished her on the back seat of his mother's pea green Citroën, and she had turned fifteen in the bed of a dark-eyed drummer who they had all seen on television and lusted after. When they found boys of their own to slide eager hands up their skirts, Estelle involved herself with a young actress who lived in an apartment with a view of the river and who composed appalling poetry about her long golden hair and her blue eyes, about her perfect skin and how her beauty would never fade. It seemed that way to a lot of people. The worst she ever looked was tired. Even after her second overdose, when the doctors were saying they weren't sure whether or not she was going to be OK, she had looked beautiful and peaceful, as if a kiss from the right person would wake her up and everything would be fine. And when Veronique and the others were going through a phase of kissing each other because they were tired of boys, but all secretly wishing they were kissing men, Estelle became the occasional mistress of an extraordinarily well preserved middle-aged man who told her he was in a loveless marriage and took her shopping for shoes and jewellery.

Although she was always the first at everything, she had never kept her discoveries to herself. When she found the dance scene she introduced them to all the best clubs and the most amiable ecstasy dealers, and when she discovered the fun that could be had in Berlin she invited her friends to explore the city with her, and after she had a tattoo she bought them all tattoos for Christmas.

There were quite a few things that Estelle had done that they didn't particularly want to do. She had been sent to a clinic after dropping to sixty percent of the weight she was supposed to be, she had injected mountains of heroin, she had translated the complete poems of R.S. Thomas into French, and had looked on in wonder as her older brother gradually became her older sister.

Veronique had let herself drift away from her friends during her time with Jean-Pierre. She told César that the first thing she would do now she was suddenly young again would be to meet up with Estelle and see what happened. They could end up anywhere, maybe teasing grey-templed English-men in a bar on La Pigalle by pretending to be lovers, or blind drunk on Cava in a nightclub where everybody else was Spanish, or skinny-dipping in a lonely millionaire's rooftop pool.

'Whatever we end up doing,' she said to her Saint Bernard, 'it won't be sitting around getting stoned and listening to soundscapes.'

She had lost concentration, and managed to miss the turning she had been planning to take. She didn't mind. She knew where she was, there wasn't much traffic around and she was enjoying singing along with the song that was playing on the radio. The road dipped. She was entering a tunnel. Not wanting to hit the sides she drove carefully, and slowly.

CHAPTER FOUR

She woke up, with her jacket and shoes still on, to the sound of the telephone ringing in her parents' room. She slowly eased herself out of bed and went to answer it. Each ring was like having the sharp end of a pine cone pressed against her eyeballs. She picked up the receiver and tried to speak, but could only manage a low croak.

'Who's that?' came the voice from the other end.

'Me.'

'You sound dead.'

'Maybe I am. What time is it?'

'Nearly two o'clock.'

'Well it's wonderful to hear from you, but what

are you doing calling me at nearly two o'clock on a Sunday afternoon? It's much too early.'

'I didn't think you would be in this state. I thought you never went out any more. I thought you just stayed in with that Jean-Pierre, exploring the twin worlds of light and sound with your boring-old-man drugs.'

'Ah, Estelle, you are so behind the times.' She lay back on the bed. 'I've made a break for freedom. I went to his place last night, and we just sat there and we drank and we smoked, and I wasn't allowed to talk while he was playing me music that sounded like somebody sandpapering an anthill.'

She saw a stale glass of water on the bedside table, and drank it in one go.

'He still just lies on the floor, talking about his stupid plans. If he ever did anything about them it would be OK. If he really did find an apartment on the Left Bank where he could play at being Argentinian I wouldn't mind. It wouldn't be so bad to be with him if he did all the things he talks about, like arranging concerts and starting a record label and playing in a band and writing slim volumes about the meaning of jazz. But he'll never do anything interesting. He works three days a week in his stupid job on that stupid magazine that nobody reads, and that's all he'll ever do. You know, he wouldn't even take me with him when he went to review films. He said I would distract him by asking who was who all the time.'

'He has a point. You do do that.'

'But who doesn't? Films always have too many people in them. I hate films. Except good ones, of course. I don't mind them so much. Anyway, he's useless. But I don't have to think about that any more.'

'I knew it wouldn't last. After all, how many times did you go with somebody else when you were supposed to be with him?'

'Only once.'

'That's not true. I can think of at least two people you went off with, and I haven't seen you for ages.'

'OK, maybe one and a half. One of them was an ex, so he only counts as a half because I wasn't doing anything I hadn't done before. Oh, and there was another one, but he only counts as a half too because he was just a friend I got drunk with one night. So three really, but I'll say two. Which isn't bad for eight months. It's almost married.'

'If you say so.'

'But enough about me. What about you? What have you been up to?'

'This and that. Things got a bit hectic for a while, so I had to go to the countryside for a few weeks to calm down.'

She knew what this meant. Sometimes Estelle's brain turned into a kaleidoscope and her parents would drive her to a cheap private hospital in the countryside, and leave her there for as long as it took to get her back to normal.

'You should have called. Or somebody should have. I would have visited you.'

'No, it was nothing this time. I just needed space to breathe, and anyway I got to spend some time on my Welsh. It's been getting a bit rusty. I'm almost like a normal person these days, you know. I'm working in a fancy boutique, and living with Brigitte and her guinea pigs.' Brigitte was her sister. 'Her flatmate got sort of married and moved out so she had a spare room. It's worked out fine, apart from the fucking guinea pigs. Anyway, we're both back from the wilderness, so let's go out.'

'When?'

'Tonight.'

'Where shall we go?'

'What kind of a question is that? Who cares where we go?'

'But it's Sunday – maybe things will be quiet.'

'You sound like boring Jean-Pierre. There's always fun happening somewhere, and we'll find it, and if we can't find it we'll just have to make it ourselves. Have you got a car at the moment?'

'Yes, my parents'. They're in Benin for the next three weeks, seeing my brother and his wife and their excellent babies, so César and I have got the house and car to ourselves.'

'Pick me up at eight, OK?'

'OK.' She paused. 'Estelle?'

'Yes?'

'It's so good to hear from you. I was thinking about you yesterday, after I left Jean-Pierre. You were the first person I thought about. I was going to call you as soon as I had come back to life.'

'Spooky.'

'But seriously, I've really missed you and I feel terrible that I haven't been in touch for such a long time.' Her shame was magnified several times by her hangover.

'OK,' said Estelle, 'you're talking shit now. Go back to sleep, and I'll see you later.' She put the phone down.

Veronique lay back on the bed, and thought about her drive home from Jean-Pierre's. Suddenly it seemed as if the room had entered a new Ice Age. She remembered the crash.

She walked downstairs and through the kitchen to the garage, and looked at the car. The panel on the back left-hand side, where the other car had hit hers, was dented, and the brake light was smashed up. She didn't know what to do, so she went back to the kitchen, where she drank another glass of water and fed César. Then she went back to bed, telling herself she would think about it later.

*   *   *

She woke up to find a message on the answer-phone. She must have slept right through the ringing. It was from Jean-Pierre. 'I am going away today for about a week,' he said, slowly. 'I am going to my mother's. Don't call me there.' There was a long pause. 'Her number is . . .' He read out the number of his mother's apartment in Marseilles. 'But don't call me.' The message ended. Veronique thought for a moment, then pressed *delete*.

She sat down and flicked on the TV. It was nearly four o'clock. She felt a bit better now, but she still wished she hadn't carried on drinking after she had got home. She half-heartedly vowed never to drink again. The news was on. There was a shot of the horribly mangled wreckage of a big black car. Then there was somebody she recognised as Prince Charles standing outside a hospital. Then there was a still photograph of Princess Diana. She started listening to what was being said, and she realised what she had done.

'Oh shit,' she said. 'I killed the princess.'

CHAPTER FIVE

Veronique opened the front door. 'Come in,' she whispered. 'Quickly.' She bundled Estelle inside. 'You didn't tell anyone, did you?'

'What, about how you killed Princess Diana and her boyfriend?' Veronique had called her after seeing the news, and begged her to take the Métro to her house as soon as she could. She had assumed Veronique had been having an episode, and would calm down after a glass of wine and, maybe, a slap. They had a long-standing agreement that if one of them was to become hysterical then the other would be allowed to slap their face to bring them to their senses. They had seen this strategy work effectively on television plenty of times.

'Yes,' whispered Veronique. 'Obviously. So did you tell anyone?'

'No, of course I didn't.'

'So you didn't even tell Brigitte?'

'Not even Brigitte. And even if I had she wouldn't have listened. She's only interested in her guinea pigs, and her clothes, and her beautiful boys.'

Veronique wasn't listening. 'What am I going to do?' she asked.

'First of all, have a drink and calm down.'

She recognised this as sound advice, and they walked through to the kitchen. 'So are you clean at the moment?' she asked, as her shame at her neglect returned. She had a guilty look on her face, a bit like César had whenever he was caught having disgraced himself on the carpet.

'Completely. I'm still off the heroin. It's been a year and a half since the last time, and I'll never take it again. It's just so bad for your skin. And I limit myself to just one pill at parties now – and anyway I've hardly been to any parties since I came back from the countryside, and all I drink is fruit juice. That's pretty clean if you ask me.'

'And what about the poetry of Wales?' asked Veronique. The day Estelle had finally given up heroin she had found an English language anthology of poems from Wales, and had fallen head over heels in love with every one of them.

'I can't say I'm entirely clean when it comes to the poetry of Wales,' she said. Her eyes misted over. 'There will always be a piece of my heart that belongs to Dylan Thomas, and R.S. Thomas and all the other Thomases.' Knowing that if she didn't check herself she would carry on forever, Estelle stopped talking about the poetry of Wales. During her last stay in hospital the other patients had ended up presenting her with a petition begging her to limit her recitals and her proclamations on the subject to just one hour a day. Every patient had signed it – even those who usually did nothing but rock backwards and forwards and moan had somehow managed to muster the wherewithal to put pen to paper in protest, and even some of the nurses had signed it. She started concentrating on opening a bottle of wine.

'I thought you only drank fruit juice,' said Veronique.

'Grapes are fruit, aren't they?'

'I suppose so. Let's sit down and I'll tell you all about it.' Followed by César, they took their glasses through to the living room.

'It all came back to me in a flash,' said Veronique. 'There I was, going home after that boring night I told you about. I was driving *so* slowly and *so* carefully, because I knew I was drunk and stoned at the same time. I went into that tunnel, the one on the news, and I saw these bright headlights coming from behind me really fast. The other car wasn't slowing down and it looked as if it was going to just blast on past me on the inside lane, but I wouldn't let it because it was being so rude. I moved into its path to teach it a lesson, but instead of slowing down like it was supposed to it seemed to speed up even more. I tried to move out of its way but it hit me and I wobbled all over the road and nearly hit the side of the tunnel. It was a horrible feeling, but I put my foot down and carried on, as fast as I could. I was so worried for

César. I didn't dare look in my mirror, but I heard a noise from behind, like a thud. I had the radio on – it was David Bowie singing "Heroes" – so the crash didn't seem as loud as it must have been in real life. It was a bit like that sound you get when you're parking in high heels and your foot slips and you accidentally smash the living shit out of the car behind.' Both of them knew this sound very well. 'It didn't sound that serious at all, but I heard the car beeping its horn so I guessed they must have been pretty mad at me.'

'Are you absolutely sure you're not having an episode?' Estelle remembered a particularly fun-packed weekend which had ended with Veronique spending the whole of the Sunday afternoon sheltering behind her bed, convinced that the ninety-year-old woman from across the street was hiding in a tree with a blowpipe and a quiver of poison darts, just waiting for her to come into view.

'Trust me, I'm sure. Come with me.' Estelle followed her through the door that led from the kitchen to the garage, and Veronique showed her the dent. The back lights were smashed in and the panel was a bit crumpled, but really it didn't look too drastic at all.

'This isn't so bad,' said Estelle. 'Are you sure you haven't made a mistake?'

'I'm positive. Completely. The tunnel, the time, the car . . . it was me who caused the crash.'

'Hey,' said Estelle, 'I've just thought of something.'

'What?'

'Oh fuck!'

'Thanks for that. You're so helpful.'

'OK,' said Estelle. 'This shouldn't be too hard – we just need to find a practical resolution to a perfectly surmountable situation.' They drank in silence for a few minutes. 'So when are your parents back from Africa?'

'About three weeks.'

'So it's easy. We'll get the car fixed and pretend it never happened. They'll get back from their holiday to find a perfect car and a happy, relaxed daughter, and they won't suspect a thing. Nobody will suspect a thing. There was no mention of a little white car on the news, so who's to know?'

'But I'm broke. I can't afford to get it fixed.' She was starting to wish she hadn't bought her jacket, but then she noticed it hanging magnificently over the back of a chair and the warmth she felt towards it reassured her that they belonged together.

Estelle thought for a while, and her strategy gradually started to take shape. 'Jean-Pierre smokes a lot of dope, right?'

'Yes.'

'And what do men who smoke a lot of dope all have in common?'

'I don't know.' Veronique thought for a moment. 'Bad hair?'

'No. Well, yes, they do mainly have bad hair, but they also owe their girlfriends money. All of them. They borrow money when they need it, and they never pay it back, even when they have it. They hide it away like fucked-up squirrels, petrified of a day when they won't have enough to score. So how much did he owe you?'

Estelle was, of course, right. Veronique had lent Jean-Pierre money before he started his job on the magazine and he had never offered to pay it back, even though she knew he had built up some savings. 'He owes me six thousand francs. Shit. I should have got him to pay me back, and then left him.' She told Estelle about the bundles of notes she had seen in a drawer in his bedroom.

Estelle rolled her eyes. 'Let's go over there now and get it from him.'

'We can't.'

'Why not?'

'He's in Marseilles, at his mother's, and I don't have her number.'

'So his apartment is empty?'

'Yes.'

'And do you have a key?'

'Yes.' She hadn't thought to dramatically hand it back to him as a symbol of the finality of her decision.

'OK then.'

'What?'

'Problem solved.'

'How?'

'Er . . .' Estelle waved her right hand in a circular motion, as if she would elicit the obvious that way. 'Empty apartment,' she said. 'Drawer full of money,' she said, still waving her hand as though she were reeling in a particularly dim-witted fish. 'You have the key,' she said. She stopped waving her hand, and started pulling at her hair in desperation. When that didn't work she started pulling at Veronique's hair in desperation.

'Ah,' said Veronique, finally making sense of what Estelle was on about. 'I see. You're *so* bad. No, we can't do that. It's out of the question.'

'OK, we won't then.' She let go of Veronique's hair and smiled. 'But tell me again – who was it who killed the princess?'

'Shit,' said Veronique. She looked at the wall, biting her lip and knocking her knuckles together. 'OK. We'll do it. Listen, let's go tomorrow. It's too late now. Stay here tonight and help me drink myself to sleep.'

Estelle picked up the phone, and called the answerphone at her apartment. 'Hello Brigitte. It's the beautiful Estelle here. I hope you had a nice time at work tonight. I won't be coming home until tomorrow. I'm far too busy having the time of my life with Veronique.' She put the phone down. 'I had to leave a message. She worries about me. If she'd come home from work to find I wasn't there she wouldn't have been able to sleep, and I'd have been in big trouble. I think I'm becoming her third guinea pig.'

Veronique turned on the TV. It was full of news of the crash, so they watched a video instead. She tried hard not to think about what she had done. They started talking, about anything but cars and tunnels and dead princesses, and soon the video was forgotten and was talking to itself. César lay on the floor, and Veronique rested her bare feet on his ribs as they rose and fell in time with his snores.

CHAPTER SIX

They woke with throbbing heads, showered the layers of alcoholic sweat from their skin, argued about the best kind of clothes to wear for a burglary, drank litres of iced water laced with aspirin and called their monosyllabic bosses, pleading guts in turmoil. Then they took the Métro to Jean-Pierre's place. Neither of them said a word. They just sat there, Estelle half asleep and Veronique trying her hardest not to look too suspicious.

'Very Bohemian,' said Estelle, yawning as they reached street level and she saw the rows of modern houses, offices and apartment blocks built from boring bricks. '*Very* Jean-Pierre.'

'His place isn't so bad,' said Veronique, 'and

there's always somewhere to park, so it could be worse.' She wondered for a moment whether she would have stayed with him so long if the parking near his apartment hadn't been quite so convenient. After a few minutes they reached his building.

The aspirin and adrenaline had helped to dull her hangover, leaving a feeling she couldn't quite place. She took her keys out of her bag and opened the front door. They went up the stairs, and she put the key in the door to his apartment. Her face lost what little remained of its colour, and she took the key out again. 'What if he's in there?' she whispered to Estelle. 'What if the train to Marseilles was cancelled, and he's come back here?'

'Well,' said Estelle, 'Why not try knocking?'

'Oh, yes. I suppose I could do that.' She looked at the door without doing anything. 'But what if he answers? What if he's there?'

'Then you come clean.'

'What?' Veronique whispered, her eyes so wide that Estelle started to worry that her eyeballs would pop out of their sockets and end up dangling by their slimy strings. 'You mean tell him I killed Princess Diana? Just like that? *Oh, hello Jean-Pierre, how are you? And by the way, you would never guess what I've done!* What if he calls the police?'

Estelle closed her eyes and shook her head. 'No,' she said, trying hard to be patient. 'I didn't mean that. If he answers the door we'll just tell him we're here for the money – that we happened to be in the area and since you felt like buying some phenomenal shoes to celebrate your separation we decided to drop by on the off chance that he hadn't gone to Marseilles after all and was able to pay back the six thousand francs he was owing.'

'Ah. That kind of coming clean. OK – that's better.' Veronique was sure there were holes in this excuse, but her brain was too fuzzy to work out where they were. She was happy to hand over all the tactical work to Estelle. 'And what if he asks me to go back to him? To give him one more chance?'

Estelle ignored her and banged on the door. There was no response, so she grabbed the key from Veronique, and opened the door. They stepped straight in to the living room, and Veronique turned on the light. 'First things first,' said Estelle. 'Where's the kitchen?'

Veronique pointed, and Estelle fetched two bottles of beer.

'I thought you only drank fruit juice.'

'What's beer made out of?'

'Barley, I think.'

'Barley's a fruit.'

'I don't think it is.'

'Well, what is it then?'

'I'm not sure. Maybe it's a cereal.'

'Well a cereal is a kind of fruit. Don't you know anything? Anyway, this is a crisis, so shut your mouth and drink your beer.'

They sat on the sofa, and Estelle looked around. It was her first visit to Jean-Pierre's apartment. 'I always pictured him living somewhere arty,' she said. She had only met him a couple of times, and could only just remember what he looked like. She mainly remembered his hair, and the annoying way he would show off with his cigarette smoke. Neither the apartment nor the neighbourhood seemed to be the natural home for someone as oppressively Bohemian as him. 'But at least this place isn't full of fucking guinea pigs.'

They lit cigarettes. The coal scuttle that Jean-Pierre used as an ash tray was already full of cigarette butts, so they decided they wouldn't have to worry about hiding theirs from the police and dropped them in. The cold beer took the edge off what was left of their hangovers.

'OK,' said Veronique. 'Let's get this over with. I've never done a burglary before, and I'm not sure I'm enjoying it all that much.'

'Then why don't you just go and get the money, so we can get out of here? You are such a useless criminal.'

'OK.' She stood up and walked into Jean-Pierre's bedroom. She felt wretched. His bed was unmade. She stretched out on it, and could smell him – that blend of tobacco, shampoo and boyfriend that had become so familiar. She rubbed her cheek against the pillow and settled down, looking drowsily at the short, fine hairs she had left behind, as they lay beside the long dark hairs that he had left behind.

She closed her eyes and breathed in the scent she had so dramatically walked out on. She fell asleep.

She jolted awake as if she had been hit on the back of the head with a shovel. Estelle was calling to her, asking her if she had found anything yet. She got up and opened the drawer where he kept his money. She lifted out a load of shirts, but there was no money there. She tried the other drawers, but none of them contained his savings. She lifted his mattress and looked underneath. She looked in his cupboards.

'Shit,' she said to herself, because there was no money. 'Shit,' she called to her friend in the next room.

They started hunting through drawers in the other rooms, looking behind books and CDs and under lamps and chairs. Half an hour later they had found nineteen cigarette lighters, six socks, two decks of pornographic playing cards and something that looked a bit like a potato peeler. They found seventy-three francs in a mug, but there was no wad of notes.

'So what do we do now?' asked Veronique.

'Well he owes you money, right?'

'Er . . . yes.'

'So we'll get it from him in another way.'

'And this other way that you mention . . . does it involve breaking the law at all?'

'Not really.'

'So what you're really saying is that it does.'

'Well, technically there might be a slight legal transgression, but you're morally entitled to get your money back, so really I would say no. Ethically it's entirely legal, so where it matters you're in the clear.'

'Unless we get caught by the police.'

'I suppose there's a slim chance that the police would take an unethical view of the matter. But you shouldn't worry – we won't get caught.'

'How do you know?'

'I just know. Listen – how many times have I been caught stealing?'

'Twice.'

'Ah. Yes.' Estelle had forgotten about her brushes with the law. 'But apart from those two times, how often have I been caught stealing?'

'Never.'

'Exactly – I know what I'm doing.'

'So how are we going to get this money?' She was expecting the worst. She wasn't sure what the worst would be, but she was expecting it.

'Do you remember when I was a hopeless and boring heroin addict?'

'Yes.'

'Well, how did I get the money for my habit?'

'You slept with rich men quite a lot, if memory serves. I'm not doing that, and anyway I don't have time. I need money right now.'

'Yes, I did sleep with rich men, but only good looking ones. Anyway that's not what I'm talking about. I also stole things. I stole clothes, CDs, electrical things, anything, and sold them to a man called Clément. He's a nasty man with terrible hair, but he was useful to know and he paid reasonably well.'

'So . . .'

'So I'll call Clément, and he'll come round and

buy that.' She pointed to Jean-Pierre's small and expensive stereo. He tried to feign indifference towards it, but Veronique knew he really loved it to distraction.

'We can't. It would be too cruel.' She shivered at the thought. 'It would be like stealing one of his eyes, or popping his eardrums with chopsticks.' She mimed popping his eardrums with chopsticks.

Estelle shook her head. 'You are so soft. What is wrong with you?'

'But it's his pride and joy. He'll be devastated.'

'Have you forgotten about what *you've* done? And anyway, he's got six thousand of your francs. Do you think he would ever have paid you back? You don't owe him any favours – he's a shit.'

Veronique groaned, and clamped a hand to her forehead. She was desperate to climb out of the mess she was in, to forget it had ever happened and get back on with her life. 'OK, call your friend Clément.'

'Hey, he's not my friend. Not even slightly. Anyway, I'll have to call him from a pay phone

– I can't call him from here. You just sit there and wait and I'll get back as soon as I can.'

Veronique checked that the door was locked. She sat on the sofa, drinking her beer and trying not to think too hard about what she was getting herself into. Unable to relax, she got up and wandered over to César's cushion, and looked at the hairs that lay on it. They reminded her of the hairs on Jean-Pierre's pillow. She saw César's special bowl. It was big and light brown, and his name was written on it in big black letters. She wanted to take it away with her, but she knew she couldn't, that the Saint Bernard had taken his last drink from it.

She thought of the time Jean-Pierre had given her the bowl. 'I've got something for you,' he had said, and she asked him if he thought it was her birthday. 'No,' he said. 'I just wanted to give you this. For no real reason.' He had handed it over, telling her he had walked past a shop that painted them to order and had thought of her and César, and couldn't resist getting them one. His generosity and thoughtfulness had given him a mysterious and wonderful glow. He had been so different on the night she left him, so lifeless and wrapped up in himself.

The telephone rang, and she nearly died of fright. Once she realised that it was only the telephone, and not a police siren, she calmed down. She waited for the answerphone to click on. Jean-Pierre's recorded, stoned voice spoke for a while, as Miles Davis played in the background. She was relieved to hear Estelle, and she picked up the phone.

'I had to walk all the way back to the Métro to find a phone. I'm going to stand around here and meet Clément, and he's going to drive me over. He's busy at the moment, so we'll be round in about half an hour.'

'OK. See you then. Remember, it's apartment four. Ring the bell.'

Veronique pressed a few buttons to make sure their conversation hadn't been recorded, and sat down. She took some of her hair in her fingers, and started to weave a plait. She tried as hard as she could not to think about anything. Most of all she tried not to think about Jean-Pierre.

*   *   *

About half an hour, Estelle had said. So why, after just a few minutes, did Veronique hear a key scratching in the lock? Estelle hadn't taken the key with her so it couldn't be her and Clément coming to collect the stereo. She stood up and tried to run into the bedroom to hide, but her legs felt as though they were about to give way beneath her, so all she could do was stand there, her beer bottle in one hand and her cigarette in the other, and watch as the door opened in what seemed to be slow motion. She had never paid the creaky hinge any attention before, but now it was almost deafening. In spite of her fear, she practised a line in her head: *Oh Jean-Pierre, I'm so sorry about the other night. Let's get back together.* She didn't have time to think of an explanation for being in his apartment after he had told her he was going to Marseilles.

But it wasn't Jean-Pierre who walked into the apartment. Nor was it Estelle and Clément. It was somebody else. A man. A huge, unsmiling man who had to duck to get through the doorway. And when he was in the apartment he stood there, like an ice sculpture, staring down at her.

CHAPTER SEVEN

He was at least six and a half feet tall, with thick silver hair and a thick silver moustache. He moved slowly towards Veronique. She looked up at him, and he looked down at her, his eyes hooded by his enormous brow and his thick silver eyebrows. He had a bag slung over his shoulder, and was carrying a small wooden box in each hand.

She smiled, at last. 'Oh,' she said. 'Hello, Uncle Thierry.'

Saying nothing, Uncle Thierry walked around her and into Jean-Pierre's room. The door was still open from the ransacking. She stubbed out her cigarette and followed him. She leaned against the door frame and watched as he opened the shutters and stood looking out at the view. After a while he slowly put one of his boxes on the window sill, and then, just as slowly, put the other one next to it. Veronique stayed quiet. Uncle Thierry looked at his watch, and reached into his pocket for a pencil and a pad of paper. He wrote down the time. Then he put a hand on both boxes, and lifted a wire grille from the end of each one. Nothing happened, so he rapped his enormous knuckles on the top of the left-hand box. A pigeon flew out of it, and off towards the rooftops. Immediately he rapped his enormous knuckles on the top of the right-hand box, and a pigeon flew from that one too. He watched them until they were out of sight, then he picked up the boxes and walked past Veronique and back into the living room. He sat on the sofa.

Veronique followed him, and stood in front of him. 'So how are you, Uncle Thierry?' she asked. 'Are you well? You look well.'

He didn't say a word. He pulled the strap of his bag over his head, put the bag on his lap, rummaged around and brought out a plastic box. He took the lid off it and reached inside for a thick sandwich.

He unwrapped it from its foil and, very slowly but taking big bites, started to eat it.

'What's in your sandwiches today, Uncle Thierry?' asked Veronique when he was halfway through.

Uncle Thierry took another bite.

'I think I can see lettuce,' she said.

Uncle Thierry lifted up the top piece of bread and stared for a moment at his open sandwich.

'And tomatoes,' Veronique said. 'And some meat, I think. Is it ham?'

Uncle Thierry closed his sandwich and took another bite.

'Jean-Pierre's not here,' she said. 'It's only me today.'

Uncle Thierry took a bite that almost finished the sandwich off.

'Did you have a good journey?' she asked.

He swallowed the last of the sandwich, then unwrapped another one.

'Are all your sandwiches the same today, Uncle Thierry?' she asked. 'Or are some different from others?'

Uncle Thierry just carried on chewing. Usually

Jean-Pierre had been around to keep the conversation flowing. Veronique supposed she had said enough about his packed lunch.

He looked at her. 'How are you today, Veronique?' he asked quietly.

'I'm very well, thank you. It's so good to see you.' She meant it, too.

Uncle Thierry took another big bite of his sandwich.

'I'm sorry,' said Veronique, 'I almost forgot. Would you like a beer?'

He held up two fingers, and she went to the fridge. Fortunately there were three bottles left, so she opened two and took them through to him. Jean-Pierre always kept at least two bottles in the fridge in case Uncle Thierry turned up. Even when it was late and they were crying out for a last drink before bed, he would leave two beers for him, even if it meant they had to go without. She had loved watching the two men together. Jean-Pierre was so attentive and listened so patiently to his uncle, even when he wasn't saying anything. By the time Uncle Thierry had left, her heart would be so full of warmth for Jean-Pierre that it was all she could do to keep herself from proposing marriage.

Uncle Thierry drank from one of his bottles, and the doorbell rang.

'I'll go and see who that is,' said Veronique. She decided to go and meet Estelle and Clément at the main door and warn them about her unexpected visitor. 'I'll only be a moment. You make yourself at home.'

Uncle Thierry looked straight ahead, and carried on eating his sandwich and drinking his beer as Veronique rushed out on to the landing to find Estelle and Clément coming up the stairs. 'Jean-Pierre's kind neighbour let us in on his way out,' said Estelle. 'This is Clément, by the way. Clément, this is Veronique.'

'Hello, Clément.' Veronique smiled a lot more than she really needed to. She looked Clément up and down. Estelle was right – he had really, really terrible hair. His face was mean and his clothes were bad, and he looked just as she would have expected somebody to look if their job involved moving stolen property around, only with worse hair than she ever could have imagined. 'And how are you today?'

Clément had no time for pleasantries, and said, seemingly without moving his thin lips, 'So where's this fucking stereo then?'

Veronique whispered, 'Er, it's in here, but you'll have to wait a moment before buying it. We have a visitor who doesn't know about what we're up to. You're just friends of mine and Jean-Pierre's, OK?'

Clément fumed.

'No, really, it's nothing to worry about. You'll see what I mean. He'll be gone soon, and anyway it'll give you a chance to play with the stereo,' she said. Clément was used to there being lots of skinny people hanging around junkies' houses when he was doing his business, and he knew Estelle wasn't stupid enough to stitch him up with a plain-clothes gendarme. He decided that it wouldn't be such a bad idea to spend some time finding out exactly what he was buying for a change. They went into the apartment.

'Uncle Thierry,' said Veronique, 'this is my friend Juliette, and her boyfriend Simon.' Estelle gave Veronique a look that could shatter granite, and Veronique immediately regretted her joke. She felt awful for having lied to Uncle Thierry, and for having made an unfunny joke at Estelle's expense. When neither of the men were looking she mouthed a heartfelt apology, which Estelle accepted with a roll of her eyes and a shake of her head.

Uncle Thierry carried on eating his sandwich.

'Beer or wine Veronique,' barked Clément.

Veronique went to the kitchen, opened a bottle of red wine and poured three glasses, and a glass of water for Uncle Thierry, who she remembered always drank water to wash down his sandwiches and beer.

'Simon,' she said to Clément, 'why not put some music on?'

Clément, who had been eyeing the stereo, walked over to it and turned it on. There was a warm pop from the speakers, and he pressed play. Nothing happened. *Where Soundwaves Turn*

To Sound by The Sofia Experimental Breadboard Octet was still in the drawer.

'Skip to track two,' said Veronique. 'It starts very quietly.'

Clément did as he was told, and sat cross-legged on the floor. Soon a discordant hum was filling the room.

Uncle Thierry coughed for a while, then went back to his sandwich. It was his last one, and he had nearly finished it. Nobody spoke.

Finally, Uncle Thierry finished the sandwich. Estelle looked expectantly at Veronique, as if this meant he was on the verge of leaving, but he reached into his lunch box once again. He took out an apple. With all that had been going on Veronique had forgotten about the apple. He looked at it for a while before starting to eat it very, very slowly, taking big bites but chewing each chunk laboriously, as though as it were thick, rare steak. Track two had ended, and track three had begun. Uncle Thierry carried on eating his apple as the others sat around without saying a word.

'Hey,' said Estelle after a while, as she tuned in

to the melody that had risen from the murk of the soundscape, 'they're playing your song.'

Veronique didn't feel like dancing this time. The music went on, and when Uncle Thierry had finished his apple he stood up. Estelle and Clément realised for the first time just how tall he was.

'Oh, Uncle Thierry, must you go already?' asked Veronique. 'It seems as though you've only just arrived.'

Uncle Thierry looked down at Veronique. 'Thank you,' he said. 'Thank you Veronique for the beer and the glass of water.'

'You're welcome, Uncle Thierry.'

Estelle and Clément expected him to leave immediately, but Veronique knew it would take at least five long minutes. He put his empty lunch box carefully into his bag, which he put over his shoulder, then he picked up his pigeon boxes. He seemed to do everything at the speed of a glacier.

He walked to the bathroom, boxes in hand. He left the door open, and they all sat quietly as the sound of his urine hitting the water echoed around the room for what seemed like weeks.

THE LITTLE WHITE CAR

Clément forgot his anger for a moment, and marvelled at how a man could have a bladder so incredibly large, but he soon began tapping his foot. Estelle gave him a cigarette to keep him quiet. He lit it clumsily, burning its underside. He pecked at it as if it was the first time he had ever smoked, and made all kinds of unnecessary sucking and blowing noises as he inhaled and exhaled the smoke.

After four false endings, Uncle Thierry emerged from the bathroom with his boxes. 'Veronique,' he said, as she stood looking up at him, 'please say hello to Jean-Pierre from me. Please tell him his Uncle Thierry says *hello.*'

'I will, Uncle Thierry. And you have a good trip home.' She reached up and kissed him, and he walked out of the door.

'That was Uncle Thierry,' said Veronique. The others ignored her.

'OK,' said Estelle to Clément. 'Are you buying it or not?'

'Yes, I'll buy it. It's fine. The music's no good, in fact it's fucking shit, but the sound's all there.

70

I might even keep it for myself, since it's such a bargain.' He laughed. Clément had three jokes, none of which were funny, and that was one of them. He used it several times a day. He knew Estelle well enough to know not to bother haggling with her. He started to sort out the wires. 'Get some bags,' he said. 'We don't want to be seen with this.'

They tidied up, and walked towards the door. Just as Veronique was about to open it, Clément noticed César's bowl. 'Wait,' he said. He circled it twice, obviously concentrating very hard. Then he unbuckled his belt and pulled down his trousers and his faded, mottled red underpants. Taking care to position himself correctly he crouched, his arse hovering directly above the bowl. Veronique and Estelle could see his thin, red penis quite clearly. It was raw-looking, like an Arctic explorer's face, and hanging like a half-used pencil in front of a long grey scrotum.

'Er, Clément,' said Veronique, 'excuse me, but what are you doing?'

He was straining. 'What do you mean *what*

am I doing? Can't you see? I'm shitting in the dog's bowl.'

'I thought so. Just out of interest, why is that?'

He looked at her as if she was stupid. 'Didn't they teach you *anything* at school?' he sneered. 'It's just what we do, people like me.' This kind of thing was such a routine part of his day-to-day life that he hadn't really thought before getting on with it. Since his bowels weren't moving quite as smoothly as he had anticipated, he took the time to explain himself further, as though Veronique were an exasperatingly slow pupil. 'A shit in an inappropriate place will make it look more like a real burglary. He'll never suspect his so-called friends if there's a human turd stinking the place out.' He pulled an extraordinary face. 'Think about it – what kind of person would do that to their friend?' He grinned horribly. 'Think of it . . . ah,' he strained, '. . . as part of the service.'

'This is the most disgusting thing I have ever seen in my life,' said Veronique.

'You don't *have* to stand there watching. And anyway I'm doing,' he gasped, 'you a favour. Shit,

it's hard today. It must be that beef I ate yesterday. I bet that bastard butcher sold me British
beef.'

'He can't have done,' said Estelle, who didn't
seem at all surprised by Clément's *modus operandi*.
'If you had eaten British beef you would be dead
by now.'

'I suppose so.' His face had turned bright red.
'Hold on, I can feel it coming . . . Get me some
paper, it's on its way . . . Oh baby, here it comes . . .'
The wine had made him giddy, and he punched
the air with both fists. Veronique found herself
reluctantly impressed by his balancing ability.

'No, Clément, please,' said Estelle. 'It's not that
Veronique and I don't appreciate your help, because
we do, but please don't. Not today.'

Clément lowered his victoriously raised fists and
shook his head. 'Well, don't come running to me
when you get caught. I've got to go though − I
can feel it coming.' He dashed to the bathroom
with tiny steps, his trousers and underpants around
his ankles and his dappled, clenched backside on
display. He didn't have time to close the door, and

after a volley of squelches, grunts and splashes, they heard the flush.

'He's a strange one,' whispered Veronique.

'Yes, I suppose he is,' said Estelle. 'But he has his uses.'

'You were right about his hair,' said Veronique.

They both shivered at the thought of it.

They shut the apartment's door without locking it, hoping that would make it seem a little bit more like an authentic burglary, and dropped everything on the passenger seat of Clément's car. He drove away, and they walked back to the Métro. Estelle put the money in the pocket of Veronique's jacket.

'So how much did we get?' asked Veronique.

'Four thousand five hundred.'

'Ouch,' said Veronique. It was less than half what the stereo was worth, even second hand. They walked on without talking.

As they stood on the platform Veronique said 'Ouch' again. She had remembered that *Where Soundwaves Turn To Sound* by The Sofia Experimental Breadboard Octet was still in the tray of the CD player.

CHAPTER EIGHT

Veronique was glad to get home, and to have a bit of money. She hoped it would be enough for her to be able to take the car to a mechanic so she could forget the crash had ever happened and get on with starting her life without Jean-Pierre. César was delighted to see her, and she gave him a big hug. 'Oh César,' she said. 'What have I got myself into?' She went into the kitchen, and they shared a small bag of cashews. She kissed the top of his head. 'There's something I want to say to you César,' she said. 'I know that what I've done over the last couple of days – killing the princess and stealing the stereo – is really terrible. But I want you to know that none of this mess is your fault. It's all because of me, César, so you're not to feel guilty. OK?' He wagged his tail. 'I'm so sorry to have dragged you into this.'

They went outside and she watched him as he sniffed his way around the lawn. He reminded her of Uncle Thierry. She loved them both, even though she could only guess at what went on inside either of their heads. They were both far too big for their own good, and they were both almost unbelievably nice. The only real difference between them that she could see, and it was a big difference, was that César was happy, and Uncle Thierry wasn't. There was no doubt about it, she thought. Uncle Thierry was very unhappy.

She had first encountered Uncle Thierry shortly after she met Jean-Pierre. She had been lying naked on Jean-Pierre's bed in the early afternoon, kissing an equally naked Jean-Pierre with her eyes closed when, suddenly, the shutters opened. Too shocked to scream, she had frantically tried to find something to cover her body. Jean-Pierre turned to her, and whispered, 'Don't worry. It's only Uncle Thierry,' and he said it with such unexpected tenderness that she felt reassured, as if it wasn't as strange as all that to have a man the size of Mont Blanc glide silently into the room and open the shutters.

Jean-Pierre quickly pulled on a pair of trousers and a shirt, and Veronique found the duvet and wrapped herself up in it. She watched as Jean-Pierre stood quietly next to Uncle Thierry as he looked into the distance. After a minute or two the older man put the boxes on the window sill. He looked at his watch, wrote on a pad of paper and lifted the grilles. Nothing happened. He rapped his enormous knuckles on the top of one of the boxes and a pigeon flew out, making Veronique jump. She hadn't thought to expect it. He rapped his enormous knuckles on the top of the other box, and this time Veronique was slightly less surprised to see a pigeon fly out. When the birds were gone he turned away from the window.

'This is Veronique,' said Jean-Pierre, pointing. 'My new girlfriend.'

'Hello,' Veronique had said, lifting one of her

arms out of the folds of the duvet and waving it very slightly. It was the first time Jean-Pierre had referred to her as his girlfriend.

Uncle Thierry looked at her for a while. His eyes had a melancholy about them that made her think, even on this first meeting, of her dog. He said, very quietly and politely, 'Hello, Veronique.'

'I'll be back in a while,' said Jean-Pierre, and the men left the room. After a long wait she heard the roar of Uncle Thierry's urine, four false endings, some muttered valedictions and the door clicking shut.

'That was Uncle Thierry,' said Jean-Pierre, as he came back into the room and put his arms around her. She was still cocooned in the duvet.

'I know. You introduced us. Listen. Maybe it's wrong of me to ask, but what was he doing watching us?'

'He wasn't watching us. Don't worry. We might as well have been gutting fish for all he cared.'

Jean-Pierre was glowing with a warmth she had never known in him before. She kissed him. 'You must love him very much,' she said.

'I do. And so will you once you get to know him better.'

She felt she was starting to love him already. 'Does he live around here?'

'No. He lives in the countryside near Limoges, where my father's side of the family comes from.'

'And is he in Paris for a long time?'

'No, just as long as it takes him to set his pigeons flying, drink his beer, eat his sandwiches, eat his apple, drink his water and go to the toilet. He'll be driving out of the city already. He always worries that the pigeons will get home before he does.'

'Jean-Pierre,' she said, unbuttoning his trousers, 'why don't you tell me all about your Uncle Thierry? Afterwards, I mean.'

For the first time Jean-Pierre didn't light a single cigarette.

It turned out that the apartment they were in was owned by Jean-Pierre's parents, and that he didn't pay them any rent. They were divorced but got along well enough, and neither of them could face the complication of selling the place, so they left him alone as long as he kept the place in reasonable condition, paid all the bills, and accepted that Uncle Thierry had a key and could come into the apartment and into his room whenever he liked. The timing of these appearances varied because of the time of year, atmospheric conditions and the inevitable turnover of birds, but they normally happened about every two or three weeks, usually during daylight because Uncle Thierry liked to watch his pigeons until they had flown beyond the buildings and off towards their home. Jean-Pierre was content with this arrangement, and was happy to accommodate his uncle.

Uncle Thierry, Jean-Pierre explained to Veronique as she played with his chin, pinching it to make a cleft and then wobbling it about, was his father's younger brother. He had been very handsome as a young man, and funny and popular, and when he was twenty years old he had fallen in love with a beautiful girl of sixteen from his village. Her name was Madeleine and she had, it seemed, loved him just as much as he loved her, so he couldn't believe it when, after two years of romance, he heard from a local gossip that she had been seen through a window in an embrace with a short, balding man who had come to their village on business from Lyon. Uncle Thierry confronted Madeleine, asking her whether it was true, and she confessed. She said she was sorry, but that she didn't love him after all, that she didn't know why because he was tall and handsome and funny and her friends and family were all very fond of him, but she couldn't escape the truth – she had fallen in love with somebody else, this strange little man from Lyon.

'You've seen my uncle,' said Jean-Pierre, 'so you know he's big, and even though she knew he was gentle she had never seen him upset before and was worried. She was very small and she thought he might lose his temper and hurt her, but Uncle Thierry has never hurt anybody. My father later heard from the girl's family that he had said, "I forgive you, Madeleine. But please will you do one thing for me. Please, when you marry that man, would you move to Lyon and stay there with him. I couldn't bear to see you walking around this village with children that aren't mine."'

She had agreed, and four months later she and

the other man were married and living in Lyon, a long way from Uncle Thierry. When they visited the village they arrived late at night and stayed inside her family's house or in the back garden, where there was no risk of being seen by those dark, sad eyes.

'Poor Uncle Thierry,' said Veronique.

'Yes. He took it very badly.'

'So what happened next?'

Jean-Pierre told her how, as soon as he had said those words to Madeleine, Uncle Thierry had gone to see a man in the village who sold pigeons. He bought two and took them home in a cage, and then he worked through the night and into the next day building them an aviary, where he kept them for a few weeks before putting them in their boxes and driving them to Paris. Once he got to Paris he visited Jean-Pierre's mother and father, who were living in the apartment, and quietly asked if they would mind if he let his pigeons fly from their bedroom window. They said that would be fine. A while later he was back again to do the same thing. Then, after the time when they had been out at the theatre and had come home to find Uncle Thierry waiting outside in his car, they gave him his own keys and told him that in the future he could come and go as he pleased. They weren't to know that from then on he would simply walk into the apartment unannounced and go straight to the window whether they were there to answer the bell or not, but they didn't have the heart to stop him.

'My father once asked him why he had become so preoccupied with pigeons,' said Jean-Pierre. 'He had only really meant why pigeons in particular and not something else, like brewing beer or growing giant vegetables, but Uncle Thierry took his question the wrong way. He said, "Because I need something to think about without stopping. From the moment I set the pigeons free I think about them on their flight home, and as soon as they arrive home I prepare for their next flight, and I think about that very hard. Please don't ask me about this again. Please just let me do it." And Uncle Thierry, who had been such a joker, such an intelligent and happy young man, has done nothing since but release his pigeons from that window, drive home and sit there, looking into the sky and waiting for them to return before getting ready to drive here and start the process all over again. When he comes here I ask him about his sandwiches, or the journey to Paris, and sometimes he'll tell me a little bit about them, and I ask after his pigeons and he'll sometimes tell me in a few words about problems with their health, or how long it took them to fly home the last time, or how one never made it home at all, but I know he doesn't want to talk about anything else. I don't press him, because even talking about nothing much at all is very hard for him.'

'Does he have no interests at all apart from his pigeons?'

'At Christmas and on his birthday we'll give him a jigsaw puzzle or a set of oil paints, or something like that, but we know he'll never touch them, that they'll just sit there in the corner of his room.'

'Poor Uncle Thierry.'

'Yes. Poor Uncle Thierry.'

'And poor Madeleine.'

'What do you mean *poor Madeleine*?'

'Well, imagine having to live your life knowing that you've destroyed somebody in that way.'

'She didn't have to go off with that other man.'

'She was just a girl. Can't you forgive her?'

'It's hard when you see what she did to him.'

'Uncle Thierry forgave her.'

'I know, but he's too wonderful to have not forgiven her. And he loved her so much, how could he not forgive her? But, as you say, I suppose she was just a girl.'

'Do you know what became of her?'

'She and the man from Lyon divorced after a while. She regretted the marriage and they had no children. Nobody told Uncle Thierry. Then she married somebody else, a very rich man. She was incredibly beautiful – I've seen a photo of her – and still young. They had two children, two boys. Nobody told Uncle Thierry about that either. She died in a road accident six years ago. Nobody told Uncle Thierry.'

'Poor Uncle Thierry,' said Veronique.

'Yes,' said Jean-Pierre. 'Poor Uncle Thierry.'

*　　*　　*

'Come here César,' she called. The dog came over to her, and she scratched him behind his ears. 'I'll miss Uncle Thierry,' she said. He was one of the things she hadn't thought about as she had left Jean-Pierre. It hadn't been an impulsive decision, but it had started to seem like one, as if she hadn't really weighed up the good things about their relationship. She had thought only of the nights spent inside getting stoned and listening to boring music when they could have been out having fun and living life, of the monologues about plans that would never come to anything, and of the way she had grown so indifferent to his voice and his skin and his hair. Jean-Pierre had been so different when his uncle had visited, and the effect lasted for hours, and sometimes even days. He had given her and César the bowl not long after one of these visits. This glow always faded, and he would inevitably become the same stoned and ineffectual Jean-Pierre, but if Uncle Thierry had visited him on the day he had played her *Where Soundwaves Turn To Sound*, there was no way she would have left him, and there was no way she would have driven through that tunnel. She would have spent the evening curled up with him, happy to listen to whatever nonsense he felt like playing on his small and expensive stereo.

For as long as she had known Uncle Thierry she had wanted to tell people about him, about his pigeons and his sandwiches and about how wonderful he was, but she could never find a way of describing him that would do him justice, so she never told anyone about him, not even her family or her closest friends. She kept him secret from everybody, in case the words she chose made him sound like nothing more than a strange old man. She had never taken his photograph. She had wanted to, every time she saw him set his pigeons flying. She had wanted to travel with him to his village outside Limoges and take photographs of him as he looked out at the empty sky, to produce a set of pictures that would capture the sadness and wonder of the man. She had never known how to ask him, and now it was too late to even think about it.

CHAPTER NINE

At work Veronique made a point of not mentioning that she had killed Princess Diana at the weekend. She had practised not mentioning it as she took César for his morning walk, and all the way to the office – on the street and in the Métro. She decided that the best strategy would be to not say anything at all, in case a confession were to slip out by mistake, like the time she had meant to discreetly clear her throat in a restaurant and ended up coughing an oyster into the middle of the cheese board.

She sat at her desk, switched on her computer and watched her reflection as it came and went in the changing colours of the screen. She became convinced that she had an instantly recognisable look of guilt about her. She tried to relax the muscles in her face, hoping the look would go away, but this only seemed to result in her looking even more guilty than before, so she tried to stop looking at her reflection altogether and think about other things.

Usually she would try to combat the tedium of her job by talking about anything that came into her mind with anyone who would join in, so after a while her silence was noticed by the other people in the office, not least by Françoise, the woman who had the desk next to hers and who wore the most irritating clothes in Paris. Veronique often wondered where Françoise had bought her billowing lime green blouse with its giant lilac bows on the shoulders, or her strawberry-print trousers that looked as if they were on back to front even though they weren't, or her shoes with pom-poms on the toes, or her belt that was as wide as a human hand and covered in pictures of teddy bears. Veronique never saw these clothes anywhere but on Françoise, and she couldn't begin to imagine a shop anywhere in the world, let alone in Paris, that would have the bare-faced audacity to sell them. She could feel Françoise's eyes boring into her, and knew that it was only a matter of time before she said something.

'You're quiet today,' she said, with an air of faux concern.

Veronique didn't much care for talking to Françoise on a good day, and today she cursed her all the more for sitting so close. She had no choice but to answer. 'I'm still a bit unwell. You know – from yesterday.'

'Ah, yes. Yesterday. I remember yesterday. Your terrible stomach pains. We were all *very* concerned for you.'

Veronique wondered why Françoise couldn't just be nice. 'There was no need,' she said, trying hard to rise above it. 'Really, it was just one of those things. I'll be better in a day or two.'

'So did you do anything at the weekend?' Françoise asked, clearly suspecting that Veronique's day off must have had something to do with some kind of rampant excess, and wanting to get to the bottom of it.

'No, not really.'

'You must have done *something*.' Françoise's already narrow eyes narrowed even further. 'Everyone does *something* at the weekend.'

'I didn't do very much at all.'

'So you just stayed in?'

'Yes, more or less. I walked César a few times, but mainly I just stayed in. And then I started feeling ill.'

'So you didn't take any of your photographs?'

'No.' Veronique's hackles rose. She hated talking about her photography at work. She wished she had never told any of them about it. Every moment spent in the office was a moment that could have been spent out with her camera. She didn't like to be reminded of that, particularly by her colleagues, all of whom – even the ones she got on reasonably well with – seemed to be united in their belief that photography was nothing more than pointing a lens at something and pressing a button, and that anyone could do it if they could but be bothered and remember to keep the sun behind them. After her first exhibition she thought she had made it, that she would be able to make a living out of photography from then on, but even though her work had been well received, commissions came in too slowly, and when they did the small magazines that ran her pictures took months to settle their bills, and when they finally paid up she would have to spend all the money on film and paper and batteries and things like that, and she was lucky if she broke even in the long run. She did this job because she badly needed the money. Every month she handed over half her pay to her parents, who had helped her out of so many tight spots with hatchet-faced landladies, incandescent vets and questionable mechanics that she had run up quite a bill with them, and they had decided that the time had come for her to pay them back. When she had been with Jean-Pierre she had taken far fewer photographs than before, and had only made half a dozen sales, all of them small. She tried to blame him for that, as if she had somehow absorbed his inertia, but she couldn't quite manage it. She knew it was her own fault.

'So you just walked your dog?' Françoise shook her head. 'What a way to spend a weekend at your age. If I was your age again I would be out having fun with boys.' Veronique couldn't imagine Françoise ever having been her age, or ever having had fun with boys. 'So you didn't even see your Jean-Pierre?'

'We broke up.' Veronique had told herself that she wouldn't mention this at work, that it was none of their business, but Françoise's interrogative assault had worn her down. And anyway, her break-up hadn't quite reached the top of her list of things-not-to-talk-about-at-work, so her preparation had been somewhat scrappy. 'Yes, that's what I did at the weekend, Françoise. I broke up with my boyfriend. Are you happy now?'

'Yes. Very happy.' She felt vindicated, having been absolutely sure that there had been more to Veronique's day off and strange mood than boring stomach pains. A terminated pregnancy, an arrest or a drug-related hospitalisation would have been better than a break-up, but she was satisfied. 'Thank you. It's heartbreaking news, of course, but at least you're young enough to find somebody new. Not like me.' Françoise launched into a routine about her collapsing marriage and her erratic weight that Veronique had heard a hundred times before. She knew she was safe. Françoise had her taste of blood, or so she thought, and would leave her alone, at least for the time being. As the rant went on, Veronique tuned out and imagined for a moment how Françoise might have reacted if she had confessed to the drunken accident and the burglary. She smiled to herself.

'Don't smile,' snapped Françoise, who Veronique suddenly realised was still mid-spiel. 'There's nothing to smile about.'

Veronique spent the rest of the day shuffling things around, and achieving very little. After lunch she noticed that her plant, Marie-France, had begun to wilt. Guilty at having neglected her, she walked over to the sink and half-filled a coffee cup with water. She walked back to her desk, and poured the water into Marie-France's pot. 'There you are,' she said.

She sat down, and looked at her photo of César.

'Don't worry, baby,' she whispered. 'Mummy will be home soon.'

'They can't hear you, you know,' said Françoise, who had been watching her every move. 'Pot plants and photographs don't have ears. You're just talking to yourself.'

Veronique remembered all the things she had told herself on the way to work, and said nothing.

'Well?' asked Françoise.

'Well what?' she mumbled, without looking in Françoise's direction.

'Aren't you going to ask me what *I* did at the weekend?'

Veronique was too exhausted to struggle. 'What did *you* do at the weekend, Françoise?'

She smiled her awful smile, and said, 'Nothing much.'

CHAPTER TEN

Veronique tried hard to think of a mechanic she hadn't fallen out with. She could think of nasty ones who she had lost her temper with when they tried to charge her much too much money for simple jobs on the various atrocious cars she had driven into the ground over the last three or four years, and nice ones who she had been so slow in paying that they had ended up having to turn nasty just to get the money they were due. Wanting to find a place that was fairly local, so she wouldn't have to drive her battered car too far, she decided to take César for a walk around the streets to see if she could find a panel beater somewhere in the neighbourhood who wasn't likely to chase her out of his yard with a spanner in his hand.

A few streets away, on a route she rarely walked because there weren't too many convenient places for César to go to the toilet, she passed a promising looking yard. Their slogan, 'We Will Fix Your Car If You Want Us To', was painted badly on the gate, and it gave her some reassurance that she had come to the right kind of place. She went in to see what could be done.

Nobody was around, so she waited. She filled the time by patting César on the head, kissing him, and telling him over and over again how good he was. Then a man appeared, as if from nowhere. His hands were black and his face was smeared with grease, like camouflage. He was wearing filthy blue overalls and a badly frayed red baseball cap, and had a thick, tatty roll-up hanging from the corner of his mouth. He stopped some distance away, and looked in Veronique's approximate direction without saying a word.

'Hello,' said Veronique, smiling.

The man said nothing. He just adjusted his

baseball cap, letting a lock of dirty blond hair fall across his forehead. She decided he would be exactly the kind of person she could trust to do a very good job on her car.

'It's a lovely day,' she said. It was, too. The sun was starting to go down behind the buildings and trees.

The man took an abnormally long drag on his cigarette, and squinted at her. 'Why are you here?' he mumbled eventually, looking at her through the smoke.

'It's about my car,' she said.

He took another long drag on his cigarette. It seemed to go on for minutes. Veronique decided he must have very big lungs. 'What car?' Slowly he looked around the yard. 'I don't see a car.'

There were cars all over the place, but she knew what he meant. 'No. That's because I didn't bring it with me. It's at home.'

The man looked mystified. 'Why didn't you bring it with you?'

'Because it's not very well, and I don't think it would be a good idea to drive it around.'

He picked a piece of tobacco from his teeth, rolled it on to his tongue and spat it on to the ground. He nodded slowly to himself, as if deep in thought. 'I see. It's all becoming clear now.'

'Is it?'

'Yes. There's something wrong with your car, and you're here because you would like to talk to somebody about getting it fixed.'

'Yes.' Veronique wondered why on earth else she would be hanging around in a place like this talking about cars that can't be driven, but she didn't want to start an argument so she kept quiet.

'You could have said that in the first place.' He adjusted his baseball cap again. 'It would have saved us both a lot of time.' He tried to take another long drag on his cigarette, but it had gone out. He pulled a Zippo from the pocket of his overalls, and re-lit it. As he huddled over the flame and shielded it from the breeze, Veronique hoped his oily face wasn't about to catch fire. 'Don't you think?'

'Yes,' she said. 'I suppose it would have done. But luckily we got there in the end. Phew!'

'So this car of yours – this broken car you keep

talking about – are you ever going to tell me what the problem is? Or are you just going to stand there with your dog, talking about the weather?'

'It's terrible,' said Veronique. 'I woke up this morning and somebody must have driven into it in the middle of the night and smashed up one of its back corners. The lights have been knocked out, and it's all dented,' she said. She bit her lip. 'Do you think you could help me get it fixed? I would be ever so grateful.'

'I'm busy now,' he mumbled. 'As you can see.' He took another long, slow lungful of smoke, and said, 'Give me your address and I'll come and look at your car when I'm not as busy as I am now.'

She fumbled in her bag and tore a strip from her cigarette packet. She wrote her address on it, and handed it over to him. He glanced at it before stuffing it into his pocket. In very few words they arranged to meet on the Sunday afternoon, so he could look at the damage and give her a quote.

'Can I have one of those?' he asked, pointing a blackened finger at the torn cigarette packet as she went to put it back in her bag.

'Of course.' She held the packet out to him, and he took one. He slowly sniffed it up and down, as though it were a Cuban cigar, rather than the second cheapest cigarette on the market, and put it behind his ear.

'I'll smoke it later,' he said, adjusting his cap once again. Veronique calculated that the cap must have rotated a full three hundred and sixty degrees during the course of their short conversation. He looked at her intently, curling his lip, and she realised that he must have taken a shine to her, and that all this time he had been trying his hardest to create an atmosphere of erotically charged conflict that he hoped would turn to rampant sex in a Portakabin. He wasn't doing an especially good job of it, but she found his ineptitude quite endearing and for a moment she wondered if he was wearing anything under his filthy overalls. 'Quite a bit later,' he said, curling his lip even more and revealing a missing canine, ' . . . if you know what I mean.'

'Yes.' Veronique had no idea what he meant, and it was clear that he didn't either, but she didn't care because it looked as though she had found a person who would fix her Fiat for her.

She steered César back in the direction they had come from and walked away, happy that everything seemed to be working out.

She smoked a cigarette, and assessed her situation. She was fairly sure she would have enough money to be able to fix the car, and that it would be ready by the time her parents came back from Benin. She had got away with it. Nobody else would ever know what had happened that night in the tunnel except for Estelle and César – the two people she could trust most in the world. She had been keeping up with the news and there had been no mention of a little white car being involved in the crash.

She made herself a coffee, lit another cigarette, yawned and turned on the television. As usual, somebody was talking about the crash. A man spoke for a while about the tunnel, about the photographers who were said to have been chasing the car, and about how England had run out of flowers. Then he started talking about some flakes of paint that had been found at the scene, and how the search was on to find the driver of a white car that looked as though it had been involved in the accident.

'Ah shit,' she said. 'Shit shit shit shit shit.'

She reached for the telephone.

'Shit,' she said, as it was ringing at the other end, probably waking up the guinea pigs. 'Shit shit shit shit shit.'

PART TWO

CHAPTER ONE

They stopped crying when Elton John came on. 'Look,' said Veronique, pointing at the television, her voice hoarse from all the sobbing. 'It's Elton John.'

They dried their eyes on their sleeves, and sat quietly as he sang. When the song finished Estelle, mad with rage, turned to Veronique and said, 'That was terrible. An abomination. The worst thing I have ever heard in my life.'

'I know,' said Veronique. 'Why couldn't he have played "Rocket Man"? That would have been much better.'

'But did you hear the words of that song he just sang? "Goodbye England's rose". *England's* rose? She was the Princess of *Wales*. Elton John should be guillotined. When I'm the elected president of an independent Wales I'll refuse him entry to my country.' She held up her hand. '*Sorry Elton – you're not coming in.*'

They stopped complaining about Elton John and went back to watching the funeral service. It wasn't long before their eyes were once again full of tears. At the end, as the coffin began to make its way out of the church to wherever it was that the princess was going to be buried, Estelle switched off the television. 'OK,' she said. 'That's enough of that. Let's get back to work.'

As sad as they had felt watching the funeral, they agreed that prison could teach Veronique nothing she hadn't already learned – she would certainly never be driving around off her face on drink and drugs again, not if things like that were going to happen. The whole situation had a sense of un-reality about it, and they still couldn't quite equate what they had seen on television with Veronique having made a slightly eccentric journey home. But they could think about that another time – there was nothing they could do to change the past, and their priority had to be staying out of trouble.

Estelle had come up with the idea of dismantling the car piece by piece, and gradually dropping the bits all over Paris – in litter bins in parks and on streets. They planned to take César on a lot of walks in a lot of neighbourhoods and take a bag or two with them each time. At first this had seemed like a great idea – the ideal way of getting rid of the evidence as the parts discreetly, almost invisibly, joined the endless stream of rubbish heading for the tips. That way, if the police came round it would seem as though there had never been a little white car in the garage, so it couldn't possibly have been Veronique in the Pont L'Alma tunnel. But, as the project went on, Veronique had started to think that maybe this wasn't one of Estelle's best-thought-out plans after all. Some bits of the car proved very easy to reduce to parts small enough to stuff into carrier bags, and their work had started efficiently as the window winders were unscrewed, the top taken off the gear stick, the windscreen wipers snapped off, and the rear view mirror unbolted. They rescued the road atlas and ate the boiled sweets they found in the glove compartment, they smashed the windows with hammers, knocked off the wing mirrors with a mallet, and collected the debris with a dustpan and brush. The headrests slipped easily from their holes, and they cut through the seatbelts with a bread knife. The trouble was, all this progress only seemed to have resulted in a lot of bags full of plastic, glass, seat stuffing and bits of random trash. The car was still the same size as it had always been, it was full of parts that would be very difficult to get at, like the steering wheel and the doors, it still had a big, heavy engine inside it, and even though they had prised the badge off, it was still very obviously a white Fiat Uno.

Estelle had a spanner in her hand, and was trying to unbolt the driver's seat. She didn't seem to be having a great deal of luck. 'I don't want you to get into trouble over this,' said Veronique, looking at her as she snarled at the stubborn bolt. She had turned up early that morning and worked non-stop except for the funeral and a trip to the park with César. She hadn't complained once, and had even worn bad clothes for the occasion – torn jeans and a curiously patterned shirt left behind by one of her sister's many lithe but empty-eyed young lovers. Brigitte had told her that he had gone home bare-chested, too stupid to realise that he was half naked. 'What if the police turn up and find you dismantling a white Fiat? They're going to think you were involved in the crash.'

Estelle shrugged her shoulders. 'I'll get out of trouble somehow. I usually do.'

'But this isn't like shoplifting, or that time you were caught urinating in broad daylight behind an apple tree in the Luxembourg Gardens. This is bigger than that – you won't be able to just say *sorry* and look a bit guilty, and get off with a slapped wrist. If I get caught that's fair enough – I deserve it – but I don't want you being arrested for being an accessory to British treason. They'll probably hang you, knowing that lot.'

'Nobody's going to get caught. But, if it makes you any happier, if the police turn up I'll just tell them you asked me to dismantle the car, and that as a friend I did it without questioning you. A perfect, watertight explanation.'

'But is it really watertight? In real life, if a friend asked you to dismantle a car, wouldn't you ask them why? Just out of curiosity?'

'I suppose I might.' She thought for a while. 'OK – I'll tell them you asked me to help you dismantle the car for charity.'

'But why would anybody dismantle a car for charity?'

'Haven't you ever heard of a sponsored car dismantling?'

'Er . . . no.'

Estelle looked incredulous.

'They're usually to raise money for the elderly. They happen all the time – my next door neighbour did it once, and I gave her fifty francs. Every piece of the car has to be reduced to such a size that it'll fit through the serving hatch of an average suburban home. If the police come, which they won't, that's what you told me, OK? As long as we both have the same story we'll be fine.'

'OK.' Veronique was happy to have a story ready

for when she was arrested, but wondered why she had never heard of a sponsored car dismantling for the elderly. It sounded like a great idea.

They worked on without saying much for a couple more hours, and then Veronique, her hands aching and black and her nails trashed, said, 'Enough. Enough for today. Stop right now.'

They put down their tools and surveyed their progress. It had been surprisingly good. They had filled about forty plastic bags from Veronique's mother's apparently inexhaustible collection. The problem of the car still being unmistakably car-shaped, car-sized and white was something they could think about another time. But for now they would scrub their hands, walk César and console themselves for not going out on a Saturday night by drinking too much beer and having pizza delivered.

Halfway through her fifth bottle, Veronique stopped throwing crusts of garlic bread to César, stood up and said, 'I don't care any more. I can't keep it to myself a moment longer.'

'What? Are you going to the police?' asked Estelle, hoping she wouldn't have to physically restrain her. She had taken a judo lesson once, but that had been a long time ago, and anyway she had given up and gone home halfway through because it had been too much like hard work, so she would inevitably have to resort to a slap or, if that didn't work, cosmetics confiscation. She knew Veronique wouldn't hand herself in to the police without her make-up on, particularly as there was such a high chance of her photograph being on the front page of every newspaper in the world, so as long as she was able to keep hold of her make-up bag until she snapped out of her confessional mood they would be OK.

'No, I'm not going to the police. I'm going to play my favourite record, and I don't care if you make fun of me. This is a difficult time and I need to hear it right now.' She walked over to the book shelves, removed a two-volume history of the Holy Roman Empire and there, hiding without a case, was a CD. She took it over to the stereo and put it in the disc tray. 'I've never told anyone about this,' she said. 'Except César, of course.' He was standing beside her, and she fiddled with his enormous ears. 'He knows everything about me. But since you know I killed the princess you might as well know all my darkest secrets.'

She pressed play, and watched Estelle's face for a hint of a reaction, but Estelle refused to reveal her thoughts on the matter. She just looked straight ahead. Then the chorus came in, and she sang along.

'Do you like it?' asked Veronique, surprised by Estelle's apparently positive response.

'Like it? I fucking love it.' They got more bottles from the fridge, and sang all the words, and performed the interpretive gesticulations that they had each worked out in private. Some of these interpretive gesticulations were uncannily similar. They agreed that *The Roxette Collection: Don't Bore Us – Get To The Chorus!* was, by a very very long way, the best record ever made, and vowed that whichever of them was to have a daughter first would call her Roxette. Estelle even admitted that for a long time she had been secretly planning to award Per Gessle and Marie Fredriksson the freedom of the city of Swansea in an elaborate ceremony at which they would play all their hits.

For a few songs the music of Roxette helped Veronique to forget her terrible situation, but as the album played on she ran into problems. 'Sleeping In My Car' just made her think of the time she had tried to fall asleep outside Jean-Pierre's apartment in the Fiat that was now sitting trashed in the garage, and when 'Crash! Boom! Bang!' came on she burst into tears. Estelle rushed over to the stereo and skipped to the next song, and soon Veronique was happily playing imaginary drums and punching the air on key changes, almost as if she had never killed a princess. When the album ended they slumped, exhausted, on to the sofa.

Estelle turned on the TV news. Among the footage of the funeral was a short piece about how the white paint found on the Mercedes was being analysed by experts to find out exactly which kind of car it was that had been involved in the crash – then, the reporter announced, the police would be able to step up the hunt for its driver.

'Oh great,' said Veronique. 'I can't wait for the police to step up their hunt for me.'

Some time in the early hours the conversation moved on to a dissection of Estelle's typically complicated love life. There was a halal butcher in there somewhere, somewhat predictably a drummer, the delinquent seventeen-year-old daughter of a Peruvian shipping tycoon and the usual stream of men writing her long letters offering her a new start in life. These letters usually arrived about once a fortnight, and tended to be from former colleagues, neighbours or school friends who had silently loved her and had been unable to get her out of their minds. They would go into exhaustive detail about how uncomplicated and happy their lives would be. They always saw her as somebody who needed to be rescued from herself, and the fresh start they offered her always featured a house in the countryside, a walled vegetable garden and a big friendly dog – for reasons she could never quite fathom, they almost always chose a bloodhound. She had long since given up replying to her failed white knights, and consigned their letters to a biscuit tin under her bed.

Suddenly, Veronique realised something. 'There's no such thing as a sponsored car dismantling, is there?' she said.

'No,' said Estelle. 'There isn't.'

'OK. At least I know.'

The three of them were tired after the day's exertions, and they fell asleep where they were.

CHAPTER TWO

Late the next morning, after Estelle had gone home, Veronique turned on the radio to see if there had been any advances in the hunt for her and her little white car. There had been quite a few. She heard that scientists, the police and the automobile industry had been working around the clock, and between them had established by rigorous tests and a process of elimination that the traces of paint found at the scene of the crash were almost certainly from a white Fiat Uno made between 1983 and 1987. She listened, numb, as a spokesman for the police asked the public to provide them with any information they thought could be relevant, and announced that they had already begun combing Paris, and that they would continue combing Paris, and if necessary the whole of France, until they found this dented car. She pictured herself in shackles.

Just as the report was ending, the doorbell rang. She felt this had a sense of inevitability, and was amazed by how calm she was. Expecting the police to be accompanied by photographers and film crews, she walked over to the mirror to check her hair. She quickly painted on some Touche Eclat and a bit of lipstick. She thought she still looked pretty rough, but at least she had made the effort. The bell rang again, this time with more urgency, and she walked into the hallway. She decided not to struggle – she would just serenely hand herself over, come clean about the crash, apologise from the bottom of her heart and take whatever punishment they threw at her. She only hoped they wouldn't hand her over to the English. She didn't much fancy being hung from a tree, or drowned in a barrel of water.

César had followed her. 'Goodbye, my baby,' she said, kissing him on the head. 'I'm sure your grandparents will look after you very well, and I know I'll see you again one day.'

The bell rang again, this time insistently. Surprised that her bowels weren't falling out of her body, she opened the door.

'Hello,' she said, smiling too much. 'And how are you today?'

She was very pleased with the excuse she thought of on the spot. With all the recent developments in her saga she had completely forgotten about the appointment she had made with her sullen new friend, and as he stood on her doorstep, covered in tantalising smears of motor oil, she came up with the perfect explanation – that after she had spoken to him the other day she had suddenly remembered that her Spanish second cousin Joaquim was an award-winning panel beater, and on hearing of her misfortune he had offered to fly to Paris from Estremadura and do the job for free. She begged forgiveness for not having cancelled the appointment, and as he accepted her offer of a coffee to make up for her appalling negligence, it felt like a moment of sheer criminal inspiration. She couldn't wait to tell Estelle about her progress in off-the-cuff underworld thinking.

'I'm so sorry,' she said to him, for the ninth time.

'You don't have to say that again,' he mumbled.

'I just feel so bad about it all.' She ran her fingers across his chest, and wished she hadn't obliterated her nails quite so comprehensively. 'I feel like such a terrible person.'

He pulled her on top of him, and ran a hand down her back until it came to rest on one of her naked buttocks. He squeezed it. 'You are a terrible person,' he said, looking at the wall, 'but you don't have to go on about it.'

'OK,' she said. 'I won't.'

He squeezed her buttock a bit more, and then he squeezed the other one. Then he held both her buttocks, one in each hand, and squeezed them simultaneously. They looked at each other for a while. 'There's something you should know,' he mumbled.

'What is it?' Veronique tried her hardest to look concerned. It wasn't easy with someone kneading her backside as though he were ringing out a pair of sponges. 'Are you secretly Greek?'

'No. I'm not secretly Greek. It's something else.'

'Are you an adult baby?'

He looked mystified. 'What's an adult baby?'

'An infantilist.' She had recently seen a documentary on the subject. 'They're grown men who enjoy wearing nappies,' she explained. 'Men like you.'

'No, I'm not an adult baby.'

'Then what is it? What could it possibly be?'

'I never have sex with anybody more than once.'

'But you just had sex with me three times in a row.'

'You know what I mean.' He was right. She knew exactly what he meant. 'It's one of my rules. It goes against nature,' he explained.

They did it one more time, and once again his technique was gloriously straightforward. There were no acrobatics and no fancy tricks, nothing to indicate that he had more than one item in his sexual repertoire. He just got on top of her and gracelessly gave her one. She ran her tongue over the bit of his gum where a canine should have been, and when he had finished he reached down for his overalls and got up to leave. Veronique pulled on some clothes and walked him down to the front door.

'So . . .,' he said, looking away from her. 'It is over. Finished.'

'Yes,' she said. 'Goodbye.'

'We will never see each other again.'

'No. Probably not.'

'There must be no kiss goodbye, no final embrace.'

'Fine.'

'I mean, we have just been like ships in the night.'

'Yes. Off you go now.'

'Our passion burned like a flame, but now it is dead – gone forever, never to return.'

'I know.' She edged him out of the house. 'Goodbye,' she said, and with a final push she shut the door.

She looked at the back of his head through the spy hole, as he stood on the doorstep, and realised she hadn't known his name. She smiled to herself. She had always wanted to do that, and now she had. But now she just wished he would hurry up and go away.

He stood dazed as the door slammed behind him. His plan had gone horribly awry. Instead of begging to see him again, as he had been certain she was going to, she seemed to have been impatient to see the back of him. He wondered why he had bothered with the stupid moody persona he had spent all those years so carefully, and it seemed so hopelessly, cultivating. He had thought it was working so well. The sex had certainly been a step in the right direction, but he had wanted so much more than just sex. He wanted her to love him as much as he loved her. He tortured himself with the thought that she probably would have liked him more if he had smiled a bit, and shown her how much he liked her, and nervously asked if he could take her to see a romantic comedy at the cinema. They could have held hands in the dark. But no. He had hidden his nerves with mutterings and a curled lip, and had more or less invited her to kick him out of her house and out of her life. He resolved to return with many, many flowers. Maybe he would even bring a box of chocolate treats for the enormous dog he so desperately wanted to grow to love as his own. Wiping a tear from his cheek, he walked to his van. By the time he reached it he had composed the rudimentary first draft of a couplet about the delicate beauty of her nose.

'It wasn't them that time, César,' she said. 'But they'll get me soon, and I want you to know that no matter how long I'm in prison I'll think of you all the time.' She hugged him. 'I'm sure they'll let you come and see me on visitors' day. I love you, César.'

She went back through to the garage and started hacking the foam out of the back seat of her little white car, and it wasn't long before she had more or less forgotten that she had spent most of the afternoon in bed with a stranger.

CHAPTER THREE

She said her goodbyes to César, walked through to the garage and picked a plastic bag from the pile. She looked inside and saw some shards of broken plastic from the tail lights, a mutilated wing mirror, an ash tray, a seatbelt and some foam. She left the house and walked towards the Métro, trying hard to make it seem as though she was just making a very ordinary journey to work. There was a litter bin on the corner of her street, which was where she had been planning to drop the bag. She started to walk towards it, but decided at the last minute not to leave it there. It was too close to home, and she felt as though familiar eyes were boring into her. If one of her neighbours was to see her getting rid of her bag in that way they could become suspicious and reach down and pull it out. Seeing what it contained they would of course call the police, who would march in and arrest her at work, handcuffing her and dragging her away from her desk in front of Marie-France, her boss, a delighted Françoise and all the others. So she veered away from the bin at the last minute, bumping into a very old woman as she did.

'I'm sorry,' Veronique said, lunging forward and grabbing hold of the old woman's coat with her free hand, to make sure she didn't fall over. 'I wasn't looking where I was going.'

The old woman gave her a look, and as soon as Veronique had released her, carried on her journey without a word.

There were three more bins on her way to the station, and she walked towards each of them, but they all seemed to be repelling her. She kept expecting them to sprout mouths and start cackling like cartoon villains.

She zig-zagged as far as the Métro, and ended up

taking the bag with her on to the rush hour train. As usual all the seats were taken and she had to stand as people rubbed against her, their breath smelling of coffee and croissants. It was a long journey, and at one point the train stopped between stations for five interminable minutes before slowly carrying on with its journey. She could feel herself starting to sweat.

The stop before hers was busy, and she had to step left and right and backwards and forwards as people moved around her. When the doors finally closed she looked down and noticed with horror that the bag had split. A sharp corner of the tail light, the world-famous tail light that had been smashed up by the Mercedes, had cut through the flimsy plastic and was sticking out and jabbing into the trousers of the man standing to her left. She pulled the bag away from his leg. She was far too forceful, and it swung straight into the leg of the woman standing in front of her, a woman who was almost certainly a gendarme's wife – she had that look about her. As she pulled the bag away from the gendarme's wife it went straight back into the leg of the man on her left. They quietly ignored her as she regained control of the errant bag, but she couldn't help imagining what would happen if the split was to get any bigger, if the bag was to break open and its contents spill on to the floor of the compartment. It wouldn't take long for the people around her to realise exactly what was going on. *Look, everyone*, one of them would say, probably the middle-aged man in the black leather jacket, who would have a clear view of the catastrophe from where he was sitting. *Look what's happened to her plastic bag – it's split open and everything's gone all over the floor.*

And look at what's in it, the fussy-looking woman wearing nothing but lilac would say. *It's full of foam and broken car parts. Why would anybody carry all that around on the Métro?*

Well, the grossly overweight man with the walrus moustache would say, *the only explanation is that she's trying to dispose of a car, piece by piece, without anybody finding out. But why would somebody want to do that?*

I wonder what kind of car those parts are from,

the grey-bearded Sikh would ask. *If we knew that then we would have a much clearer view of the situation.*

At this point the man with wild red hair and dirty fingernails would say, *Well, I'm an automobile enthusiast, and have been for nearly twenty-six years, and I recognise those parts as being from some kind of Fiat – probably a Fiat Uno.*

It would be the pretty student with glasses and long auburn hair tied in a bun who would pull everything together. Even though she was too shy ever to raise her hand in a seminar, she would take off her glasses, shake her hair loose, rise to her feet and cry, as if possessed by the Spirit of Justice, *Then that explains it all – it must have been her who was driving that car in the Pont L'Alma tunnel the other night.* Pointing and triumphant, she would say, *She was the one who caused that terrible crash. She killed the princess, and she's trying to get rid of the evidence.*

There would be mutters of *I think she's right*, and *Shame on you.* The emergency cord would be pulled and an impenetrable circle would form around her.

The police would be called to the train as the people in the carriage rejoiced in their proximity to a moment of history.

But the split didn't widen, and the contents of the bag didn't fall on to the floor. The train arrived at her stop, and taking care to keep the bag steady she made her way up to the street. There was a bin between the Métro and her office. She dropped the bag in it and quickly walked inside. Françoise ignored her, and Marie-France looked very well, and she started the day as usual, shuffling things around without achieving very much at all.

Halfway through the morning, Françoise asked her if she had seen the funeral on television.

'Yes, I did.'

'I cried for six hours,' she boasted. 'Six whole hours. The awfulness of what had happened just suddenly hit me – I was a wreck thinking about that poor princess.' She narrowed her eyes. 'How many hours did you cry for?'

'About one, I would guess. Only while it was on TV. Then I stopped.'

'Just one hour?' Françoise looked at her with contempt, and shook her head. 'Just one hour of tears for a young life so cruelly snuffed out?'

'Yes, just the one.'

Françoise tutted, and went back to her work.

At the end of the day, just as Veronique was putting on her jacket, Françoise called her over to her desk.

'So tell me – how are you finding your new car?' she asked, with suspicious politeness.

'It's fine. It's pretty old, but it goes well enough.'

'It's a Fiat, isn't it?'

Veronique kicked herself for having spoken about her car at work. Then she kicked herself again for ever having spoken about anything at work. 'Er . . . yes. It's a Fiat.'

'I thought as much. A white Fiat.'

'No. It's not white. It's orange. Bright orange.' Françoise had been annoying her all day by wearing bright orange lipstick and matching blusher, so it was the first colour that came into her mind.

'I could have sworn you said it was white. Still,'

she smiled. 'I suppose I must have been mistaken. If you say your Fiat is . . .' Françoise raised one eyebrow and then the other, and then lowered them both, '*bright orange,* then it must be . . .' she did the same thing with her eyebrows '. . . *bright orange.* Who am I to doubt you?' She smiled, horribly. 'I could have sworn you said it was white,' she repeated, 'but I must be getting old. It seems as though my memory isn't what it used to be.'

Veronique didn't know what to say.

'No further questions,' said Françoise. 'For now. You are free to leave.'

Veronique looked over her shoulder at Françoise, who was sitting at her desk and ostentatiously reapplying her bright orange make-up. Veronique wondered where on earth it was possible to buy such stomach-churning cosmetics. Maybe she had them flown in specially from the eighties.

All the way home she couldn't get Françoise out of her mind. She wondered if she really suspected something, or if she was just being her usual irritating self. Between the Métro and her house she looked out for bright orange cars. She didn't see a single one.

She got home to find that the police weren't waiting for her. There was something anticlimactic about that – the thought of being handcuffed and led away had started to assume a kind of inevitability. She said hello to César, who was dozing in his enormous kennel, made herself a cup of coffee and went straight out to the garage, where she carried on attacking the steering column with a hacksaw. Progress was horribly slow, and she found it hard to concentrate. It had started to seem futile. With every new piece of evidence that emerged it was looking more and more as though there was no way she could get away with it. Dismantling a car without the motivation necessary to dismantle a car was proving to be a pretty dismal task.

She started thinking about her mechanic. She decided that having sex with him had been the perfect way of drawing a line after Jean-Pierre. It had been the explosion she needed to mark the transition from her old life to the new life she would begin just as soon as she had sorted out the business with the car. Her reverie was broken when the phone started ringing. She walked into the house and picked it up.

'Hello,' she said.

'Hello,' said the slow voice on the other end of the line. 'It's me.'

Veronique said nothing.

'It's Jean-Pierre.'

'Oh.' She knew it was Jean-Pierre without having to be told.

'I'm back from Marseilles,' he said.

'Ah.'

'I need to talk to you,' he said.

'There's nothing to talk about,' she said. 'It's over, Jean-Pierre, and that's that.' Normally she might have been a bit more sympathetic, but she had far too much going on in her life to spend time being compassionate and attentive towards former boyfriends. She had a car to dismantle for a start.

'But you don't understand,' said Jean-Pierre.

'I do understand. I understand perfectly well, and you have to understand that it's over between us. My life has moved on, and your life has got to move on too. It's as simple as that.'

'But you don't understand,' he repeated.

'Please stop saying that.' She was surprised by just how upset he sounded. His voice was cracking and he seemed close to tears, but she knew she had to be firm. She had made the break, and to mark the occasion she had had sex with a greasy man who she would never see again and whose name she didn't even know, and even though she wasn't about to tell him that, Jean-Pierre had to understand that there was no going back. 'It's over between us, Jean-Pierre.'

'But you don't understand,' he said. Veronique was about to put the phone down when Jean-Pierre stopped her in her tracks. 'It's not what you think,' he said. 'It's not about you and me.' He paused. 'It's about Uncle Thierry.'

Veronique's blood ran cold. 'What about Uncle Thierry?'

'He's dead.'

CHAPTER FOUR

Veronique had once begun a romance with her upstairs neighbour just two days after his wife had dropped dead without warning at the age of twenty-eight. Capitalising on Veronique's sympathetic embrace, he began to make love to her with a passion she had never known. He flipped her into all kinds of extraordinary positions, he gasped, he sighed and he yelped with the ecstasy of it all and then, the moment it was over, he fell into her arms and, between sobs, told her all about how his wife's eyes had been the brownest he had ever seen, how her otherwise straight hair had curled at the nape of her neck, and how cruel the world was for having taken her away from him. Then as soon as he was ready, and it didn't take very long, he started all over again, licking her nipples with an almost unbelievable fervour, quivering, and squealing like a stuck pig. And when he was finished, he fell back into her arms and wept.

This pattern continued, and after a week of it Veronique was exhausted and decided that she had endured enough – after all *he* was the one with the unbearable reality to escape from through sex, and she was starting to find the whole business pretty tiresome. Feeling too sorry for him to leave him on his own, she had handed him over to Estelle, who had been moping around after her latest razor-cheeked boyfriend had been deported back to Estonia, or wherever he had come from. Estelle lasted for just three days before giving up and passing the widower on to their friend Phuong, who had never had sex before and had no idea that this kind of love-making wasn't normal. The novelty of it all carried her along for about a month, but after that she was so worn out that she felt she had no choice but to introduce him to her recently-divorced cousin who had been worrying that she would never have sex again. Within a fortnight Phuong's cousin had decided that maybe never having sex again wasn't such a bad idea after all, and had passed him on to a friend from work. Veronique had lost track of him after that, but as far as she knew he was still out there somewhere, moving from bed to bed, losing himself in the moment and yelping and quivering with joy before collapsing, and sobbing something only just comprehensible about how it felt as though his heart were crumbling to dust, how he would never be able to kiss his wife's little knuckles again, or how they had never had a chance to say goodbye.

She knew exactly what was going to happen when she got to Jean-Pierre's apartment, and when he opened the door she didn't say a word. She just took him by the hand and led him to the bedroom, where he quivered and gasped, and pawed her with an urgency she had never known in him, and when it was all over he put his head on her belly and cried his heart out for Uncle Thierry.

*   *   *

They pulled on some clothes and sat on the sofa drinking wine. 'Do you want to talk about it?' asked Veronique.

'No,' he said, 'not really.' But he told her everything anyway. 'It was terrible. My mother's friend from Uncle Thierry's village called her while I was in Marseilles. They told her that he had been behaving unusually for a few weeks. He had been going into the village every day to buy wine – the only alcohol he had ever been known to drink before had been the occasional glass of something with a meal, and the bottles of beer I would give him on his visits here, but he started buying three or four bottles of wine at a time, and taking them home. Once he was even seen walking unsteadily though the village late at night. Everybody was worried sick about him, but they didn't know what to do.'

'Did you have no idea this was going on?'

'None at all. Nobody thought it was their place to talk to us about it, and anyway he always had regular visits from the family, so I suppose they assumed we knew what was happening. But whenever any of us visited he seemed just the same as ever. Nobody noticed him acting out of character, and nobody saw any wine bottles lying around. I suppose he must have hidden them away if he knew we were coming. Anyway, a couple of weeks ago Uncle Thierry's trips to the shop to buy wine stopped, and everybody was very relieved – thinking it must have been a phase that had come to an end. But last Thursday they heard a gunshot from the direction of his house. This was long after dark and all the children were in bed, so everybody was surprised by the noise. Some men who had been drinking in a bar grabbed a torch and raced over to see what was going on, but more shots rang out and by the time they got there it was too late. He was in the aviary, lying on his side.'

Veronique didn't know what to say. She took Jean-Pierre's hand and waited for him to carry on.

'Nobody knows where Uncle Thierry got the revolver,' he said, 'but he had fired six shots – the first five blowing the heads off all five of his pigeons, and the sixth going straight through his heart.'

Jean-Pierre stopped talking, and Veronique put

her arm around his shoulders. She felt wretched. The last time she had seen Uncle Thierry she had lied to him, and wished he would hurry up and go away so she could carry on with stealing his nephew's stereo.

'I have something to tell you,' she said, looking at the floor.

'What is it?'

'You can be as angry with me as you like, I don't mind. I deserve it.'

'What is it?'

'It's about Uncle Thierry.'

Jean-Pierre said nothing.

She took a deep breath. 'He asked me to say hello to you. He said, *Please tell Jean-Pierre that his Uncle Thierry says hello.*'

Jean-Pierre stared at the ceiling. Veronique held her head in her hands and closed her eyes.

They stayed like that for quite a while.

'Did you drive over tonight?' asked Jean-Pierre.

'No. My car's not working,' said Veronique.

He thought for a long time before asking her, 'What kind of car is it again?'

'A Fiat. A Fiat Uno.'

'A white one, right?'

She nodded.

'I thought so.' He carried on staring at the ceiling. Veronique didn't know what to say.

'So how much did you get for it?'

'I haven't sold it – it's in the garage.'

'I didn't mean the car. I meant my stereo.'

'Ah.' She wasn't going to pretend she didn't know what he was talking about. 'Four thousand five hundred,' she said.

'I bet you could have got more than that for it. I owed you six thousand. We'd have been even if you'd got six thousand for it. I still owe you one thousand five hundred.'

'You don't owe me anything. I'm so sorry.' She felt too guilty to look at him.

'Don't worry about it. You were desperate.'

'How do you know I was desperate?' she asked.

'Well,' he said, 'I think I would be pretty desperate if I had just killed a princess.'

When he had heard about the white Fiat on the news he had wondered, just for a moment, whether

Veronique had been the driver. He had tried to work out if she would have been on the road at that time, but had given up before long. After all, she had just left him and he had gone all the way to Marseilles to try and forget about her, but her car's confinement to the garage, her meeting with Uncle Thierry that could only have happened in his apartment, the clearly uncoincidental disappearance of the stereo and her sudden desperate need for cash led straight to the truth. 'You're in deep shit, aren't you?'

She nodded.

'I mean really deep shit.'

She nodded again.

'Why don't you tell me all about it?'

She confirmed what Jean-Pierre had already worked out, and told him all about her increasingly disheartened attempts to get away with it. The only part of the story she left out was the afternoon she had spent with the mechanic. She thought that maybe this wasn't the right time for that particular anecdote.

'So do you still have the money from the stereo?' asked Jean-Pierre.

'Yes.'

'But instead of spending it on fixing the car you're going to have to put it towards buying a whole new car by the time your parents get back from Africa. Is that right?'

'Yes.'

'But before you can get a new car in the garage you'll have to get rid of the old one without anyone noticing. No?'

'Yes.'

'I'll tell you what.'

'What?'

'I'm glad I'm not you.'

As if somebody had flicked a switch, his eyes filled with sadness, and he lunged towards her and plunged his tongue into her ear. He bucked and whinnied like a startled pony, and afterwards he put his head on her belly and cried his heart out for Uncle Thierry.

'Stay here tonight,' he said.

'I can't. I've left César in the garden.'

'Then can I go back to your house with you?

You can show me the car, and we can walk César together in the dark. I've missed him.'

'Have you really?'

'Of course I have. I've missed both of you.'

'But aren't you mad at me for what I've done?'

'Yes, a bit. Quite a lot, in fact. But I'll get over it.'

'Thanks.' She smiled. 'Of course you can come back with me.'

The strange thing was, she felt she wasn't taking him home out of pity, or out of a sense of duty, or in gratitude for him not calling the police. It was much, much stranger than that. She was taking him home because she wanted to.

CHAPTER FIVE

'Right,' said Veronique, throwing down her screw-driver. 'That's decided then.'

'What's decided?' asked Estelle, as she swept car-scrapings from the garage floor. She had no idea what Veronique was on about.

'I'm going to London.'

'Oh. Why are you going to London?'

'To get my toe cut off,' said Veronique.

'OK,' said Estelle. 'Off you go then. I'll see you when you get back.'

About a year and a half earlier, Estelle and Veronique had gone to London to visit their friend Phuong, who had been staying there for a few months studying dinosaur bones. On their first night they had gone to a party at the house of one of Phuong's fellow students. Most of the conversation had, as is usual when Englishmen are involved, revolved around the eating of horses and the force-feeding of geese. Englishmen always seemed to mistake the French girls' polite smiles at these topics for genuine amusement, and they somehow managed to convince themselves that they were in with a chance of a bit of *ooh-la-la*, as they insisted on calling it. Estelle and Veronique had been to the city before, and were quite used to the locals' idiosyncratic idea of a good night out, so for both of them it was just another London party in a shared rented house a long walk from the nearest bus stop, and where everything seemed to be either sludge brown or nicotine yellow, even the whites of people's eyes. They were quietly making plans to salvage something from the evening by kidnapping Phuong and sneaking off to a club when the doorbell rang and a new guest turned up.

'I'm sorry I'm late,' he said to the party's host,

as Veronique's ears tuned in, 'but things were really hectic at the hospital.'

Suddenly petrified of anyone else getting in there before her, she raced up and introduced herself. 'Hello,' she said. 'I'm Veronique. I'm from France.'

Her English was fairly good, but his French was better. He explained that he had learned the language at school and had spent a year with *Médecins Sans Frontières*, so the two of them spoke mainly in French. After about an hour she crept away from him and took Estelle and Phuong to one side.

They had both long since abandoned the plan to move on somewhere else. As Veronique had been busy advancing on her quarry they had found a game of table skittles set up in the corner, and begun to play. It wasn't long before they found themselves becoming quite involved in the whole thing as Phuong started thinking tactically, and Estelle began playing with increasing aggression. They considered their vague enjoyment of the game to be a triumph of the human spirit in the face of extraordinary adversity – like when prisoners of war passed the time by playing whispered games

151

of chess with neither board nor pieces, relying on their minds to hold every move in place. Even so, by the time Veronique reappeared they felt they had played enough for one session and were content to sit and listen to her.

'Life is wonderful,' she told them.

'And why would that be?' asked Phuong, who knew exactly why.

'Well, you're born. Then you go to school. Then you leave school with hardly any qualifications, not because you're stupid but because you didn't concentrate in class and in the evenings you had better things to do than homework. Then you go on a photography course, just for something to do, and find you're quite good at it. Of course along the way you learn a lesson or two, like just how big Saint Bernards really are, or that chickens don't eat cheese, or that sometimes you have to work in a boring job to make a living. Things like that. These are hard lessons, but they help you to grow from a girl into a woman. You meet a few boys – some you stay with for a while, and others you get rid of as quickly as you can. And then, when you're twenty-one, you meet a handsome young doctor in London, you fall in love and you marry him. Easy. Anybody who says that life is complicated should shut up because they don't know what they're talking about.'

'So do you like him?' asked Estelle. 'Is that what you're trying to tell us?'

'Yes. I think he's very nice.'

'And are you going to see him again?'

'Of course. In fact we're going out together tomorrow afternoon – he's taking me out in a boat on the Serpentine, whatever that is. I'll see him a few more times while I'm over here, then I'll have to go home to get ready for my exhibition and to care for César.' She sighed. 'Of course it'll be hard for us to bear being apart, so he'll come and visit me in Paris, and after a while he'll invite me to move in with him in London, and I'll say yes, even though I'll be going to visit César and oversee my many high-profile Parisian exhibitions for a few days at least once a fortnight, and then we'll get engaged. You two will be my bridesmaids – what would you like to wear?'

'So do you really think this could be something

serious?' Estelle looked concerned, as she tried her hardest not to picture herself in a bridesmaid's dress.

'Yes. I think it could be. In fact I know it's going to be serious. He obviously adores me, so I don't foresee a single problem.'

Neither Phuong nor Estelle seemed convinced that Veronique's romance was going to be quite so free of trouble. They didn't know what to say.

'Aren't you happy for me?' asked Veronique, noticing their serious expressions.

'Well, it's not that we're not happy for you. Of course we're delighted for you. It's just . . .' Estelle didn't know how to put it. She started fiddling with the skittles.

Phuong helped her out. 'The trouble is, he's English.'

'I know he's English. After all we're in England, and it's not as if he's been trying to hide that from me. So what's the problem with him being English? You two have spent more time in London than I have, and you've always gone on about what a great place it is to meet men.'

'Yes, but not *English* men,' said Phuong. 'London

is full of foreigners like us – looking beautiful and having excellent sex – but never, ever with Englishmen.'

'Well who with then?'

'Other foreigners – Paraguayans, Siberians, Irishmen, Polynesians, Micronesians, Eskimos, Kenyans, Italians, Libyans, Kurds . . . Anyone, really – but *never* Englishmen.'

'Never?'

'Well . . . some people have been known to. I won't mention any names, but it's the kind of mistake you only make once.'

'But why is being with an Englishman such a mistake?'

'Let's just say they don't exactly make the best boyfriends.' Estelle and Phuong looked at each other and smiled knowingly.

'Well my doctor is different. We talked for ages and he didn't mention geese or horse meat once. And look . . .' Suddenly amazed, as if *aurora borealis* had appeared before her in this brown London house, she pointed at him over on the other side of the room. 'He can even dance.' She put her hand over her mouth with the shock of it. It was the first time he had taken to the rug by the bricked-up fireplace that had become the dance floor. The three of them watched as he moved around to the music, and Estelle and Phuong had to concede that he was unusual for an Englishman in this respect. He danced exceptionally well.

'Well good luck,' said Phuong. 'I hope it all works out for you.'

'Yes, good luck,' said Estelle. 'Just don't ever tell us you weren't warned.'

Noticing many female eyes on her incredible dancing doctor, Veronique went over and joined him in case he was snatched from under her nose.

A couple of days later Phuong went back to her old bones, and Estelle took the train to Wales to see some poetry readings in arts centres and public libraries, to fill the gaps in her Gorky's Zygotic Mynci record collection and to fruitlessly pester the admissions tutor at Lampeter University into letting her on to a course. She told him, quite honestly, that she had been declared a genius in eight separate intelligence tests, but he was unimpressed by this statistic and kept asking her for exam certificates that she just didn't have – mainly because she had never sat an exam in her life. He did concede, though, that he was very impressed with her grasp of Welsh, and that he had never heard anybody curse quite so eloquently in the language after just six weeks of self-tuition. In the meantime, Veronique and the doctor were seeing a lot of each other. They went to dinner, they saw the sights of London, they went bowling, they saw plays, they played air hockey, and they danced. Then Veronique had to go back to Paris to look after César and set up her exhibition.

The trouble was she didn't find it nearly as hard to leave her doctor behind as she had hoped she would. She had wanted it to feel as though her heart were being torn from her body, but as they said goodbye all she thought was, *Well that was nice, and I'll see him again soon.*

She tried as hard as she could to keep the dream alive. She shuttled backwards and forwards between London and Paris, leaving César in the care of her increasingly disgruntled parents for days and sometimes even weeks at a time, but she gradually began to accept that there had been a lot of truth in what Phuong and Estelle had said, and after almost three months of clashing teeth, clumsy embraces and ill-timed declarations of love, she made one of her trips back to Paris and almost accidentally went to bed with a French boy whose lips knew exactly where they were going, and whose hands flew across her body like butterflies. When it was over she kicked him out of her room and felt miserable.

The couple who lived next door to the doctor's family while he was growing up had gone out dancing at least once a week. Sometimes opportunities to dance came naturally, as invitations to weddings and silver anniversaries and fortieth birthday parties arrived, but in the weeks when there were no such invitations they would go to supper clubs or ballroom dancing classes, or just down to the local palais where, surrounded by people half their age, they would dance to the latest songs. They didn't mind where they went, just as long as they went out and danced together at least once a week. And when the dancing was over they would go home, laughing and holding hands like teenagers.

The doctor had never seen his parents dance. At weddings and silver anniversaries and fortieth birthday parties they always sat at the back of the room, regarding the dance floor as though it were quicksand. He had been thirteen when they had separated, and he blamed everything on their refusal to dance. If they had gone out dancing once a week like the people next door, or maybe just every once in a while, then the sparks of love would never have left their marriage.

On the day they sat him down with his brother and sister and told them all that their separation had been a success, that they were still very good friends but they were going to get a divorce, the doctor decided on two things. First he was going to learn to dance like a demon, so when he met his future wife their love would stay alive, and second he wasn't going to have a girlfriend until he had found the one he was going to marry. He couldn't bear the thought of loving somebody and having that love come to an end. He was sure he would know when he had met his girl. He would shiver, and hear the sound of bells.

And so he danced, ignoring the taunts of the boys who found out about his foxtrot classes at the church hall and his appearances at the after-school disco dancing lessons that had traditionally been female-only territory. He picked up, maybe by osmosis, that women are fond of doctors, that the combination of perceived compassion, earning potential and the inevitable maternal approval was irresistible, so to increase his chances of meeting the girl he would love forever, and who would love him in return, he specialised in sciences, found weekend work as a cleaner in the local hospital, and went straight from school to medical college, where he worked hard and did well but still found the time for his dancing.

He kept himself so busy that he only occasionally noticed that he never seemed to meet the girl with whom he was going to spend the rest of his life. He told himself that he didn't have the time for romance, and that once he was established in his profession and was able to relax a bit he would be in a much better position to meet and get to know his future wife. He never had a shortage of dancing partners, but as he flung them around the dance floor he never felt the shivers he wanted to feel, and he never heard the bells that he knew would herald the first day of the rest of his life. Once the dancing stopped, many of these girls stayed around and waited for him to ask them out, but he never did. A lot of them were very pretty and very nice and he got along with them perfectly well, and afterwards he would try to work out why they were not the one. It was never easy, and he always found himself trying to blame something like the colour of her eyes or the pitch of her voice, but deep down he always knew it was none of those things – that it was the failure of the bells, for whatever reason, to ring, and if the bells weren't ringing then it would never be the grand passion that would last a lifetime. If he couldn't see himself and the girl dancing together into their old age then he saw no point in pursuing a romance.

As years went by and he failed to find a girl-friend, his friends and family began to worry about him. When he was twenty-six his mother, thinking it odd that she had never had a prospective daughter-in-law to scrutinise, sat him down and talked very earnestly about how if he had *chosen* to live his life without a girlfriend then that would be fine. She took pains to tell him that his sister had provided them with a pair of beautiful grandchildren so he was under no pressure to have children of his own. She told him that above all she wanted him to be happy, and that she would always love him *no matter how he chose to live his life*. He had shrugged off this line of conversation and quickly changed the subject. When, two years later, he told her on the telephone that there was somebody he would very much like her to meet, she had been somewhat crestfallen when he told her it was a beautiful girl from Paris called Veronique. She had spent years rehearsing for the day when he would introduce her to a José, a Michael or a Roy, and announce that they were very much in love, and she felt a little cheated by this beautiful Veronique character from Paris. All her planned conversations with her friends in which she would casually and affectionately say of her son, *Oh, he's gay, you know*, went up in smoke, and she almost lost her temper with him. But she didn't. She told him she was very much looking forward to meeting his Veronique, and by the time the girl arrived at the house in her enormous trainers and with her long brown hair tied in plaits, the doctor's mother was quite used to the idea of her son having a girlfriend. She even found herself liking the French girl very much as she played with the family spaniel and smiled politely at her ex-husband's jokes about eating horses and force-feeding geese. And on that day the doctor knew for sure that his search was over. The bells that had started ringing the moment he saw his girl at the party hadn't stopped ringing since, and right then they were ringing louder and clearer than ever before.

That night they made what he was convinced must have been the sweetest love ever made, and the next day, after he had seen her on to the train home, he went straight to a jeweller and chose a beautiful and expensive diamond ring. He had been saving for it since the day he started his first Saturday job at the age of fourteen, and as he emptied his special building society account he knew in his heart that the time was right.

Veronique felt that a letter or a phone call would be too cruel, and that she owed it to him to tell him to his face that everything was over. She arrived in England a week later, just as they had planned, with a short and simple speech prepared. He had told her to expect a surprise when she arrived. She was hoping it would be something uncomplicated, like three dozen roses.

He was waiting for her at the railway station, and he kissed her and took her bag, and they walked a few blocks to his car. They set off for his mystery destination. She had meant to tell him straight away that they needed to talk, but he was so explosively pleased to see her, like César whenever she came back from a trip, that she just didn't have the heart. She listened as he told her about what he had been up to while she had been gone, and asked her questions that were easy to answer, about her photography and about César.

Every once in a while he would reach over and pat her leg, or squeeze her hand. Veronique thought that it probably wouldn't be wise to tear his world apart while he was driving, so she decided to wait until they had reached wherever it was they were going, and then she would take him to one side.

She had absolutely no idea where they were, but after about an hour and a half he drove down a long farm track and into a field. And there, waiting for them and ready to go, was a hot air balloon.

Never having been in this situation before, Veronique had no idea what to do. She knew she should say something, but she couldn't begin to find the words. Silently, she let the doctor help her into the basket.

'Isn't it beautiful?' he asked, as they hung hundreds of feet above the ground. It was a clear day and they could see for miles.

'Yes,' said Veronique, quietly. 'Very beautiful.'

'Pardon?' The breeze had carried her words away.

'Yes,' she shouted.

'I never told you I could fly one of these things, did I? I wanted it to be a surprise.'

The doctor put his arm around her, and kissed her cheek. He rested his chin on top of her head, and they stayed like that for a while, looking out at the view and saying nothing.

'Veronique,' he said, suddenly spinning her around to face him. 'There's something I want to ask you.'

She couldn't bear to see him looking so appallingly happy. 'No,' she said. 'Let me say something first.' The words sounded awful, and his expression turned to one of horror, because he knew exactly what was about to happen.

Two hours later the balloon touched down in the middle of a big field, and Veronique at last knew for sure that he wasn't going to leap out and land somewhere in the English countryside, a mangled mess of despair, leaving her floating in the air for the rest of her life. He sat on the floor of the basket, his face buried in his hands.

She had no idea where she was, or what you were supposed to do once your balloon had landed. Everything she had brought with her, including her passport, was in the doctor's car, so all she could do was wait quietly until he pulled himself together. She looked at him. 'I'm so sorry,' she said, and she meant it. She hated herself for what she had done.

He looked up at her, his eyes red and his whole face, even his forehead, damp with tears. 'There's no need to be,' he choked.

She knelt down and put her arm around him, and he recoiled from it as though it were an electric eel.

'Please don't do that,' he said.

She stood up and moved to the other side of the basket. She wanted to say something else, but his face fell back into his hands and she supposed she should just keep quiet.

After a while she noticed a group of people approaching from the far side of the field. As they got closer she recognised them as the doctor's family. His mother was there, and so were his father, his brother and his sister, the spaniel and some people she recognised from photographs as cousins, nieces and nephews, and a few other people of various ages, presumably in-laws, stepmothers, great-aunts and people like that.

There were about twenty of them in all. They smiled and waved, and Veronique weakly raised her arm in return. 'Your entire family is here,' she said.

'Right,' he said. He wiped his eyes, and jumped to his feet. He waved at them too, and tried to smile as if nothing was wrong, but as they approached they realised that perhaps the flight hadn't gone quite as well as he had assured them it would. They all hung back a few yards, except for his mother, who charged up to the basket. Her face turned pale, and ignoring Veronique she spoke to her son. 'So did she say *no*?' she asked.

He shook his head.

'So she said *yes*?'

He shook his head.

'Then what happened? Don't tell me you were too frightened to ask her.'

'I didn't have a chance to ask her. I was about to, but then she came out with a speech about how wonderful she thinks I am, but how we just aren't right for each other. She told me there was nobody else, but she had found herself missing her dog when she was in London more than she missed me when she was in Paris.'

Veronique had meant that as a straightforward explanation, but it sounded awful the way he said it.

'And then she said that I deserved someone better than her, and . . .' When he was unable to carry on, she was quite relieved.

His mother was virtually hysterical by this point. 'But what about the ring?' she shouted. 'If you show her the ring then maybe she'll change her mind. Go on. Show her.'

He fumbled in his pocket and pulled out the tiny case. He held it towards Veronique and flipped it open.

She had no idea what to say. The ring was fantastic, and part of her wanted to try it on. 'I'm so sorry,' she mumbled.

'You don't have to be,' he said, wiping his eyes and putting the ring back in his pocket. 'It's just one of those things.'

'Well,' the doctor's father chipped in, from the impromptu camp the family had made a few yards away with their picnic rugs and folding chairs – they had been sitting there not knowing where to look, and trying to pretend that none of this was going on, 'I didn't carry an ice bucket across a field for nothing. Anyone for a drink?'

Amid the sound of popping corks, Veronique scrambled out of the basket. 'There you are, my love,' said the doctor's father, walking up to her and handing her a plastic cup of champagne. 'Get that down you.' She knocked it back in one, and he filled it straight back up. 'The course of true love,' he said, chuckling, rolling his eyes and shaking his head. 'The course of true love . . .'

CHAPTER SIX

Estelle went upstairs and watched Veronique stuffing things into a suitcase. 'I know it's none of my business,' she said, 'but just why is it that you're going to London to have your toe cut off?'

'Because even if we get rid of every little scrap of that car I'm still going to have to replace it.'

'Yes, of course you are. But when your parents get back from Africa and find that instead of a car in the garage there's just the severed toe of their daughter – pickled in a jar, perhaps, or dried and mounted in a display case, don't you think they might notice? Might they not wonder why there's a disembodied toe where there should have been a hatchback?'

'No. That's not how it works.' She carried on distractedly filling her bag.

'So how does it work? Please explain.'

'Do you remember that doctor I went out with for a while?'

'What, the English one? *The bells . . . The bells . . .*'

'Yes, him. Anyway, I remember him telling me that if you went to a certain hospital in London they would hand you over to some student surgeons who would cut off your little toe, then sew it back on for practice, and then they would give you two thousand pounds. That's about twenty thousand francs – add that to the stereo money and I can buy a whole new second hand car, and I'll hopefully even have enough money left over to buy us both new sets of nails.'

Estelle looked down at her hands. Even though they had started wearing gardening gloves while they were working on the car, they had long been obliged to acknowledge that their nails had pretty much had it for the foreseeable future. 'That doesn't seem like such a bad idea. But let's take five minutes to think about it in detail.'

'I've already thought about it in detail. It'll all be fine.'

'Just five minutes. Come downstairs and have a drink.'

'First of all,' said Estelle, 'let's look at the practical side of things. So which hospital is it you're going to?'

'I don't know. The doctor will tell me.'

'So you're going to get back in touch with him?'

'Yes. I'll go to his flat when I get to London.'

'And what are you going to say? *Hello again. Sorry about all that business in the hot air balloon – oh, and by the way where do I go to get my toe cut off?*'

'Yes, something like that. I can work out the finer details on the train.'

'But how do you know he'll be ready to help you out?'

'Because he told me he would. He told me, with tears in his eyes, that if I *ever* needed him for *anything* he would be there for me. And he meant it – I could tell.'

'But how do you know he still lives in the same place?'

'Because he wrote his address in the birthday and Christmas cards he sent me, and he would definitely tell me if he moved – he lives in hope of me changing my mind and going back to him.'

'So when you turn up on his doorstep you'll fill him with false optimism.'

'I know it's sad, but this is a crisis. Anyway, I'll make it very clear that he hasn't got a chance of getting back with me. I'll tell him the moment he opens the door, to avoid any confusion. It'll be tough for him, but the kindest way.'

Estelle was frustrated that she didn't seem to be getting through, and was beginning to feel twitches in her slapping hand. 'And what if he's not there? What if he's on holiday? What if you go all the way to London and just have to come straight back home? You'll have wasted time and money.'

Veronique clutched her forehead and groaned. 'Maybe my planning hasn't been up to much, but I still think this is my best option. You don't have to worry about me – the operations are very safe. They sterilise the hacksaw and everything.'

Estelle had once been within moments of selling all her blonde hair to a backstreet wig maker, so she had an idea of what Veronique was going through, but she was sure they would be able to find a solution without having to go to such extremes. 'Here's what you've got to do,' she said. 'First, call the doctor. Make sure he's in town and if he is, discreetly find out if there's a chance of him being able to book somebody into the toe hospital. Don't let him know it's you who wants the operation, unless he can do it – you mustn't arouse his suspicions unnecessarily.'

As Estelle had planned, Veronique began to think seriously about the reality of reappearing in the doctor's life. She pictured him opening the door to her. Maybe he wouldn't have shaved since that terrible day in the countryside. What if she found him hollow-eyed and emaciated? She felt awful, but she had spent days trying to work out how to raise the money to get out of her situation, and the quick fix of a toe operation was the best solution she could think of. In fact, with a credit history as disastrous as hers the toe option was really the only solution she could think of, apart from smuggling heroin in her natural crevices, and she wasn't about to do that. But Estelle was right – she couldn't just turn up unannounced. 'OK,' she said. 'I'll call him.'

She found his number, and dialled. The phone rang at the other end, and her heart jumped as somebody picked it up.

'Hello,' the voice said. It was unmistakably the doctor.

Veronique froze. She couldn't work out why she was so shocked by him having answered his own phone.

'Hello?' the doctor said.

'Ah,' she said at last. 'Hello.'

'Veronique?' he said. 'Is that you?'

'Er . . . yes. Hello.'

'It's so good to hear from you. How have you been?'

'I've been very well, thank you.' She felt awful about what she was doing. He sounded so relaxed, and so happy to hear from her. The effort must have been extraordinary. 'And how about you?'

'I've been very well too, thanks. Really, really well.'

'That's great,' she said, knowing it wasn't true.

'And how is César?'

Veronique remembered what she had said to him about missing César more than she missed him. 'He's very well,' she said. 'He says hello.'

The doctor laughed, and asked her to return the dog's salutations. Then there was a silence as they both wondered what to say next. The doctor broke it. 'So to what do I owe the pleasure?' he asked.

'Pardon?'

'Er . . . Why have you called me?'

'Well, I thought I would say hello and see how you are. And there's a friend of mine who is interested in having her toe cut off and put back on again. She wants to make a grand gesture for medicine.'

'Oh yes. I don't have much to do with all that any more. But if you give me her details I'll see if I can get her on the waiting list.'

'There's a waiting list?'

'Yes. They don't do the toe thing all the time. It'll probably be a few months before she gets to the top of the list. But if your friend is in a hurry to make her grand gesture, maybe she would be interested in something else, like having her eyeballs popped in and out a bit. I'm sure I can arrange that at fairly short notice.'

'No thank you. She's very keen to have her toe cut off, that's all. Her great-aunt had her finger sewn back on after a terrible accident with a cheese wire, and she was so happy with the way they fixed the old lady that she wants to help out with future operations.' Veronique remembered the toe operation being the only one that paid the kind of money she needed. Having her eyeballs popped in and out wouldn't even make her enough money for a knackered old moped, let alone a car.

'Wait,' he said. 'I'll get a pen and paper and you can give me her details.'

There was no way Veronique could wait months for the money, but she had to tell him something. So, a couple of minutes later, Estelle had a place on a waiting list to have her toe cut off and grafted back on again. She narrowed her eyes at Veronique, and took César outside to play.

'So how is Estelle?' asked the doctor.

He was told that she was very well indeed, and would be excited to hear that she was in with a chance at the toe hospital. There was another silence.

'It's so good to hear from you again,' said the doctor. Veronique was sure this would be where he would start to get sentimental, and try to convince her to get back with him. 'We should meet up one day,' he said. She had no idea what to say. She had already destroyed him once, and she didn't want to destroy him all over again. Estelle had been right all along, as usual, and she continued feeling horrible for having called him. 'Tell you what,' he said. 'Why don't you and Phuong and Estelle come over for my wedding? It'll be great to see you all.'

For a moment Veronique was stunned. Then her heart crumbled with pity. He must have met somebody inappropriate on the rebound.

'Oh. So you're getting married?'

'That's right – next summer.'

'What wonderful news. So what's her name?' asked Veronique.

They carried on talking in a hybrid of French and English, and it was half an hour before Veronique was able to put the phone down.

'Well?' asked Estelle, bringing the dog inside. 'How is your doctor?'

'He's very well,' she said, smiling just a little bit too much. 'He has a fiancée. I'm so happy for him.'

'You don't have to pretend with me,' said Estelle.

'Well I can't believe it,' she said. 'He's found somebody else, and they're living together and getting married next year.'

'So really you aren't happy for him at all?'

'Well, I suppose I am.' She shrugged her shoulders. 'Kind of. Yes, of course I'm happy for him.' Her face was like a thundercloud. 'I'm over the moon – it's fantastic news. But to tell you the truth I'm a bit mad at him too.'

'Why?'

'Well, after we split up he sent me a long letter telling me he would never love again, that he was going to devote the rest of his life to healing the sick, and that he had abandoned his quest for romance. He said he had always known that he would only ever hear the bells once in his life, and now that he had heard them there was no point in continuing his search. And what did he do just six months after my back was turned? He met someone else and started going out with her. And now they're getting married. Can you believe it?'

'OK, so he's getting married, but maybe he's making do with somebody he doesn't really love. Does he *really* hear the bells with his new girl?'

'Apparently so. He says that the bells he heard with me were like windchimes, or the gentle peal of church bells from a nearby village, but when he first saw his new girl he felt as if he was glued to Big Ben. He says he's almost deaf with love for her. And it's not just that.'

'What else?'

'He doesn't just hear bells with her. He sees shooting stars too.'

'Wow.'

'And . . .' Veronique closed her eyes and shook her head. 'There's more . . . Whenever she's near him he feels as though he's walking on air.'

'But is that really so terrible?'

'Well, as happy as I am for him, and believe me I am very happy, I'm also a little bit disappointed that he didn't keep his word.' She angrily opened a bottle of beer and drank half of it in one go.

'So what you're saying is that every man who makes a declaration in a fit of despair should stick to any promise he makes about living like a monk for the rest of his life. Yes?'

'Precisely. They shouldn't tell lies like that. The doctor should have kept his word, and that's that.'

'I know why you're angry,' said Estelle.

'I'm not angry.'

'Yes you are. You're angry because you're regretting leaving him. You gave up a handsome dancing doctor, albeit an English one, thinking you could find somebody better elsewhere, and all you managed to land was a random hippy with a gigantic saxophone who didn't even have a real job even though he was about forty. In the time you spent with useless Jean-Pierre you could have been teaching your doctor the French ways of love. He could have learned all kinds of things by now.'

'I hardly think so. And anyway, Jean-Pierre's not as bad as all that.'

'That's not what you've been telling me lately.'

'He has hidden sensitivities.'

'*Hidden sensitivities?* What's brought this on all of a sudden?'

'Nothing.'

'Are you sure?'

'Yes. Nothing.'

'Really?'

'Yes, really.' Veronique looked guilty, and knew she couldn't ever escape from Estelle. 'Except we've got back together.'

'I see, so you're back with Jean-Pierre. How romantic! And does he know about all this business?' She pointed in the direction of the garage.

Veronique nodded. 'But you don't have to worry. He won't tell anyone else.'

'I'm not worried about that. I'm just wondering why, if he's supposed to be your boyfriend, he isn't here helping us out. What's he doing? Sitting at home with his soundscapes?'

'No – we stole his stereo, remember?'

'Oh yes.'

'Anyway, he's got an excuse.'

'It had better be good.'

'He's away at a funeral.'

'Well, I suppose that's fair enough. I'll let him off. But the moment he's back in town he's coming over here and helping us dismantle your fucking car. OK?'

'He will, don't worry.'

An hour later Estelle had managed to talk Veronique into feeling at least a little bit happy for the doctor, and had convinced her that she had done the right thing in not going to London to have her toe cut off. They had even come up with a few sketchy strategies for getting rid of the car with Jean-Pierre's help.

Gazing into the middle distance, Estelle began

to recite an R.S. Thomas poem about a small boy charging around the countryside collecting snail shells, pieces of broken glass and other rural ephemera.

'Eh?' said Veronique.

Estelle recited her own French translation of the lines.

'OK,' said Veronique. 'That's very nice. But what the fuck has it got to do with anything?'

'Nothing, really. I just thought it would cheer you up.'

In fact it had the opposite effect, as it struck her that the village boy, with his pockets stuffed full of flowers, could have been Uncle Thierry in the days before his life went so badly wrong. 'Poor Uncle Thierry,' she said, and sobbed for several minutes.

She knew Estelle had been right in trying to make her feel pleased for the doctor. It was for the best that he wasn't going to sink into a life of pigeons and despair. She started to pull herself together.

Estelle resolved never to recite poetry from

Wales to her ever again if this was the kind of reaction it was going to get, and as soon as Veronique had stopped sniffing she went home, leaving her to another night of dark thoughts and fitful sleep.

CHAPTER SEVEN

There were two pieces of mail on the doormat. One was a birthday card from her parents, arriving four days early. It contained the usual greetings and a summary of what they had been up to in Benin, the time and number of their return flight, a reminder to cut the grass and hoover up all the dog hairs and, best of all, a photo of her niece and nephew playing on a slide. 'Come and look,' she called, and Jean-Pierre appeared with his hair all over his face. She handed him the photo. 'It's the babies. How cute are they?' He agreed that their cuteness transcended the realms of the subjective.

She opened the other letter and howled with delight. It was from a gallery in Madrid, telling her that they wanted to show some of her work. On a trip to Paris they had seen her sequence of twelve pictures, called *Saint Bernard: Sitting*, and wanted to include it in an exhibition of young French photographers. Each photograph featured César sitting in a different part of Paris as people went about their business around him. In some shots he was virtually ignored, and in others he had become the centre of attention. In one he was with the tourists outside the Pompidou Centre – they were gathered around him in a circle as though he were a sword swallower or a break dancer rather than a twelve-stone dog with a slightly wonky tail. in another he was sitting unnoticed outside Belleville Métro station at rush hour, and in another he was being eyed warily by unsmiling children as he sat beside a burned out motorbike in Aubervilliers. In all of them he was wearing his trademark mournful expression. The photographs had been a nightmare to take, as people she didn't particularly want to be in them fussed around him, or as he lost interest in sitting and wandered away a fraction of a second before the shot would have become perfect. But, after three weeks of trying and seventy-eight reels of film, she had twelve shots she was happy with, and now there were some people in Spain who were happy with them too.

César wandered into the hallway, apparently oblivious to his impending international fame.

She found her keys and ran through her daily checklist of the absolute essentials she needed for work: make-up, cigarettes, and a bit of money in case she ran out of either make-up or cigarettes. Jean-Pierre assured her that he would take César on a walk, mow the lawn, get rid of some of the plastic bags and carry on attacking the car. Veronique had the feeling that César's walk would consist of him being left in the back garden, and that Jean-Pierre's efforts at dismantling the car would involve more coffee and joint breaks than actual work. She was sure she would come home to an unmown lawn, a restless dog and an increasingly uncontrollable pile of bags.

As she opened the front door he called after her.

'Hey,' he shouted.

'What is it?'

'Congratulations,' he said. 'With the photos.'

'Thanks.' She smiled, and left the house.

The day passed quietly as she looked at the picture of her niece and nephew, did odds and ends of work, and tried her hardest not to throw up at the sight of the enormous purple and brown bow in Françoise's hair. She didn't tell anyone about her exhibition in Madrid. Françoise kept casting frosty glances in her direction, as if she could sense that there were secrets she wasn't being let in on.

When she got home she found the front and back lawns mown, a clearly exhausted César in his kennel, a few less bags cluttering up the garage and Jean-Pierre surrounded by recently dismantled car parts. He had taken off the doors, and had begun taking the engine to pieces.

'Wow,' she said. 'You've been busy.'

'You know me – I don't hang about.'

'Have a break. I'll make some coffee.'

He followed her into the kitchen.

'I didn't know you were a mechanical genius,' she said. He hadn't driven for as long as she had known him, and she had no idea he could even find the petrol cap on a car.

He shrugged. 'I'm just a man. And anyway the Uno isn't exactly the most complicated machine in the world.'

'So do you think we'll get away with it?' she asked.

'*We?*'

'Excuse me – do you think *I* will get away with it?'

'I don't see why not, if we work hard at it over the next few days, and if my secret plan works out. I'll have to make a few discreet enquiries and get hold of a load of tools, but I think we'll be able to get rid of it.'

'That's good news,' she said, but she still couldn't quite bring herself to believe that she would be able to put it all behind her. Even if Jean-Pierre could make the car magically disappear she would still have to buy a new one, and to stop her parents complaining it would have to be noticeably better than the car they had left behind. That was going to cost a lot more than she had.

'But what about the money?' she said. She had tried to avoid the subject as much as possible, but she couldn't hide from it any longer.

'Don't worry,' he said. 'I'll look after that side of things.'

'But how? You're as broke as I am. You haven't even got a proper job.'

'Just don't worry about it. I'll sort it out.'

She didn't want to argue, so she dropped the subject, telling herself she would raise it again later.

As soon as he had finished his coffee he went back out to the garage and carried on working. Piece by piece he carried on taking the engine apart, as Veronique wrapped the bits in sheets of *Le Monde* and stuffed them into plastic bags.

She was astonished by his dynamism. At eight o'clock she had to implore him to put his tools down for the day and come in for some food.

They sat at the table, drinking wine and picking at the remains of the meal.

'Congratulations,' he said again.

'Thanks.'

'Being chosen for that exhibition is amazing.'

'I know.' She smiled.

'Well done.' His expression changed. 'But . . . it makes me feel pretty bad.'

'Why? Why would it make you feel bad?'

He looked away. 'There's something you have to know,' he said. 'Something important.'

She had no idea what he was going to say. 'What is it?'

He looked at the wall for a moment, then stood up. 'I'm going to play you some music,' he said, quietly. He walked over to his bag and brought out a CD.

Oh great, thought Veronique. *He's going to express his innermost feelings through sound – just what I need right now.*

'What's this?' she asked, absent-mindedly lighting a cigarette as the faux-orchestral intro was joined by dramatic drums and electric guitar. 'It sounds like The Scorpions.'

'It isn't The Scorpions,' he said, even though she had a point. 'Just listen.'

She put her cigarette in the ash tray, took three strands of hair and started to turn them into a plait. She listened for hidden complexities, but there didn't seem to be any – it really was as if he was making her listen in silence to radio-friendly rock. A man who sounded as though he had enormous hair started singing in English about how somebody he loved had left him. Then came the chorus, and he sang in an almost deafening voice about how his dreams were in tatters. In the second verse he sang with great emotion about how wonderful he thought their romance had been, and how surprised he was that it had come to an end. Then there was another chorus, a massive guitar solo, yet another chorus and a key change that led into an anthemic coda backed by what sounded like a children's choir. The presumably-big-haired man told his lost love that he would do his best to carry on, even though he had cut his hands trying to pick up the pieces of his broken dreams. After a bit of apparently improvised wailing the song faded out.

He walked over to the stereo, took out the CD and put it back in his bag.

'Thank you for that Jean-Pierre,' she said.

'Did you like it?'

'Well, sometimes it's good for the soul to hear a bit of drivetime rock. Did you bring "Africa" by Toto? Or anything by Foreigner or REO Speedwagon?'

'No,' he said. 'That's the only song I brought with me.'

'And why,' she asked, still trying to make sense of his musical message, 'of all the songs in the world, did you choose to bring that one?'

'Oh God,' he said, closing his eyes.

'Jean-Pierre, is there something you would like to tell me?'

His eyes still closed, he said, 'That song you just heard . . .'

'Yes?'

'It's called "Like A Soldier (Of Shattered Dreams)".'

'I thought it might be called something like that.'

'It's number six in Germany.'

'That's great news. I'm really happy for the band, but I had no idea you followed the German music charts so closely.'

'Well I don't. Not usually at least.' He opened his eyes, looked straight at her and said in one breath, 'Please don't hate me but I wrote it.'

He brought her the occasional glass of water, and whenever her laughter turned to coughs and chokes he patted her back to keep her from dying. When, after more than half an hour, she was finally able to speak she said, 'So, you've got a big hit in Germany.'

'Yes. Well, it's not just me,' he said, burning with shame. 'I wrote it with my brother.' His older brother lived just outside the city. He mainly played the drums, and for several years he had scraped a living as a session musician and playing clubs and holiday resorts across Europe pretending to be Bev Bevan in *L'Orchestre Sous Lumière Électrique*, and both Steven Adler and Matt Sorum in *Des Flingues Et Des Roses* (he would change wigs halfway through 'November Rain'). Jean-Pierre explained that they had worked on a few songs together, mainly with him writing the lyrics and his brother writing the music on his acoustic guitar, and they had been secretly sending tapes off to bands and music publishers and record

companies for about a year, and almost out of the
blue 'Like A Soldier (Of Shattered Dreams)' had
been chosen by a German rock band. It had charted
a few days before.

'Congratulations,' she said.

'You don't mean that,' he said.

'I do!'

'But it gets worse.' Jean-Pierre hung his head.
'It's going to be released all over Europe – across
Scandinavia next week, then in Italy and Spain,
and everywhere . . . maybe even in France early
next year. And the band are considering two more
of our songs for their next album.'

'Jean-Pierre,' said Veronique. 'Listen to me.
When I said congratulations, I meant it. Congratulations – you've got a hit!'

'You mean you're not mad at me?'

'No, of course I'm not mad at you. Why would
I be mad at you?'

'Well, for obvious reasons.'

'What obvious reasons are those?'

'I didn't think you would approve of me doing
something so commercial.'

'Why not?'

'Because . . . you're exactly what I've been trying to be all my life – an uncompromising artist. And here I am writing a load of soft rock for the radio. I'm a sell-out.'

'Everybody has to earn a living, particularly at your age, and this is great. You'll make some money for the first time in your life.'

'I still wish I was more like you. Like when you sent those people packing after your exhibition – I thought that was fantastic.'

Veronique recalled the episode he was talking about. Around the time she had met Jean-Pierre, she had been approached by a couple of people from an agency. They had offered her all kinds of work – school photos, weddings, calendars, and location shoots for cheap magazines. She had indignantly turned down their offers, convinced that the warm reception for her exhibition would lead to all kinds of further lucrative outlets for her photography purely on her own terms. She decided that it would be best not to tell Jean-Pierre about the hours she had spent kicking herself for not having followed up these contacts. Every day at work she wished she had been taking photos of kittens in baskets for greetings cards, or of sixty-year-old women with their dull-eyed teen-age husbands for weekly magazines. At least she would have been out with her camera, even if she had been taking pictures of nonsense. Her exhibition in Spain wasn't even going to make her enough money to cover the cost of having taken the photos in the first place, and if she could do the photographic equivalent of what Jean-Pierre had just done – taking some unexceptional pictures for money – then right now she would do it without a thought. But of course she wasn't about to tell him that.

'I think what you've done is great,' she said. 'I'm very proud of you.'

'Thanks. But for God's sake don't tell anyone – if this ever gets out I'll never be able to show my face again.'

'I won't,' she said, smiling to herself. After all, she had secrets of her own to worry about. 'Hey.'

'What?'

'Play it again, Jean-Pierre.'

He reached into his bag, walked over to the stereo and put the CD back on. This time around Veronique was able to sing along with the chorus. It seemed strange to think that he admired her. She had always assumed that he had looked down on her as a vastly inferior being, but in fact he had respected her as an artist all this time. He had a funny way of showing it, but she wasn't going to worry about that now.

A few glasses of wine later, Jean-Pierre resumed his confession. 'You know that song I wrote?' he asked.

'Yes.' She knew it fairly well by this point. He had played it six more times.

'Do you know how I thought of the words?'

'No. Tell me how you thought of the words.'

'It was after we'd been together for about three months. I imagined how I would feel if you left me. I know it's only a stupid song, but I was so sad imagining you had gone away with somebody else.'

He had written something for her once before, but she hadn't realised at the time. They had been sitting in his apartment one evening, and he had been fiddling around on his gigantic saxophone, making vague noises. She had assumed he was tuning up, or blowing dust out of the pipes, but when he put the instrument down he turned to her and said, 'I wrote that for you.'

'It was beautiful,' she had said. 'Thank you.'

This time, though, she was really touched. It was one thing to have a load of apparently random notes played for you on a gigantic saxophone, but another thing entirely to inspire somebody to write a semi-heartfelt power ballad in your honour. It wasn't quite the ultimate compliment, but it was a step in the right direction.

'When you left me for real I felt even worse than the man in the song.'

Veronique didn't know what to say. She felt a wave of guilt, an increasingly familiar sensation, for ever having gone with anybody behind his back. She'd had no idea that she had been part of a loving relationship, and if she had done she would have been a lot better behaved.

*   *   *

'But I can't take your money,' she said. He had confirmed that his sudden financial confidence had come from the first instalment of his music publishing advance having landed in his bank account that day. It wasn't very much, but it would be enough to sort Veronique out.

'You need to get a new car, and it's the only way you'll be able to do it. How else are you going to find enough money for a car in the next few days? This is a crisis. I'm not letting you go to jail, and I'm definitely not having you rob any more of my stuff.'

'But you worked hard for it, writing all that soft rock.'

'You can always pay me back when you've got some money of your own.'

'I suppose that would make me feel a bit better about it.'

'Good. Anyway, I owe you a favour.'

'Do you?'

'Of course I do. Think about how much you've lent *me* over the last few months. I kept on asking you for money you couldn't really afford, and that I didn't really need. It wasn't as if I was starving or anything – it would all go straight to The Chinaman.' Veronique had always pictured Jean-Pierre's dope dealer in flowing robes and with a long, wispy beard, but when she finally met him he turned out to be a sandy haired man from Le Mans called Fabien who had never even left France, let alone been all the way to China. 'I feel bad about that. And anyway, I'm going to be giving a lot less money to The Chinaman from now on.'

'What, are you giving up smoking dope?'

'Giving up? No way. But I'm going to cut down. I'm only going to get stoned twice a week from now on.' He thought for a moment. 'Or maybe three times a week.' He thought for another moment. 'Sometimes four. But definitely not every day.'

Veronique was happy about that. He smoked way too much, and she was sure it had quite a lot to do with his tendency towards general boringness.

'Everything that's gone on recently has woken me up to a lot of things about my life that I need to change. I deserved to have you steal my stereo,' he said. 'It did me good.'

'No, I shouldn't have done that. I feel awful about it.' But she was happy to accept that Jean-Pierre had a point about her being able to borrow money from him without having to feel too bad about it. She had more than enough to feel guilty about without adding that to the list. 'OK,' she yawned, 'let's just get rid of the car and go shopping for another one. I'll pay you back as soon as I can.'

She slept right through the night for the first time since the crash.

CHAPTER EIGHT

'So it looks as though you're in the clear,' said Françoise, adjusting her lace-trimmed yellow nylon cummerbund. 'You must be delighted.'

'What are you talking about?'

'Apparently you're not going to be arrested after all.'

'Why was I going to be arrested?'

'For killing Princess Diana, of course.'

'Oh yes, I'd forgotten I was supposed to have done that. How come I've been struck off the list of suspects?' She tried to sound sarcastic, but was really desperate to find out what Françoise had heard.

'They've caught the driver of that white Fiat.'

'Have they really?' Veronique tried to work out how this was possible, bearing in mind she wasn't having a bright light shone in her eyes and DNA samples scraped from deep inside her rectum.

'Yes. He's a foreigner, of course – a Vietnamese. I've always said that no good would come of letting foreigners into France. Look what's happened here – you have a foreign car and a foreign driver. Put them together and what happens? A princess dies. It makes me so angry.' She seemed to have forgotten that the princess herself had been a foreigner and that her lover had been, by Françoise's standards, very foreign indeed. Of the casualties only the hopelessly drunken driver of the German car would have passed her rigorous nationality test. 'I've always said that Jean-Marie Le Pen talks a lot of sense. If he had been in power, none of this would have happened.'

Suddenly everything became clear to Veronique – Françoise must have bought her clothes from fund-raising stalls at far-right rallies. Whenever suburban fascists were interviewed on the news their innate sense of superiority would be fatally undermined by their rampant ignorance, their annoying voices and, particularly, their lack of colour coordination and commitment to nasty fabric. As relieved as she was to have solved a mystery that had been gnawing away at her for months, Veronique needed to find out more about the unlucky man who had been arrested.

'So Françoise,' she said, 'do you think they've got the right person?'

'He had a white Fiat Uno that was sprayed a different colour the day after the crash, and he is a Vietnamese. What more proof do you need?'

Even discounting the neo-Nazi element of Françoise's reasoning, Veronique couldn't work it out. She wondered if she had imagined everything, or if her accident hadn't been the famous one after all, but the more she thought about it, the surer she became that somewhere in Paris a poor, frightened man was being held in custody for no reason. A terrible thought struck her. 'What if it's Phuong's dad?' she said to herself.

'What was that? Something about somebody's father?'

'Nothing. I was just talking to Marie-France.' She patted her plant.

'You know,' sighed Françoise, 'it's Prince Edward I feel sorry for. He's such a sensitive soul – I can't begin to imagine the agony that poor boy is going through.'

'I'm going for lunch,' said Veronique, interrupting. She rushed out of the office and ran the mile and a half to Estelle's shop, glad at every step that she had decided not to wear heels that day.

As she raced along the streets, bumping into people, stumbling over kerbstones and being beeped by cars and cursed by cyclists as they braked or swerved to avoid running into her, she decided to avoid arousing suspicion by acting like any other customer at a high-class boutique. By feigning interest in the clothes, she would discreetly lure Estelle into a quiet corner where she could confide in her.

By the time she reached the shop her face was

a vivid purple and her lungs felt as though they were about to explode. She saw Estelle behind the counter, and walked up to her as casually as she could. 'Excuse me,' she said, 'I would like . . .' She couldn't get her words out, and puffed and panted for a while. 'I would like to try . . .' She bent double and wheezed, clutching her heart. She couldn't remember ever having been so out of breath, and quite a few of the browsers cast concerned glances in her direction, wondering whether somebody should call an ambulance. Then, in a single breath, she said, 'I would like to try on that dress.' She pointed vaguely at a nearby rail, and started coughing.

'Certainly, Madame,' said Estelle, picking a tiny ten thousand franc dress off the rail. 'Come this way please.'

Veronique, suffering her first stitch since school, clutched her side, moaned and bent sideways as she shuffled towards the changing rooms.

'How did I do? Do you think anybody noticed I wasn't a normal customer?' she whispered, as Estelle closed the door of the cubicle.

'You blended in perfectly. So what's going on?'

'Have you seen Phuong lately?'

'No, she's been away.'

'Where is she?'

'Ancient Egypt, I think.'

'Ancient Egypt?'

'Yes, she's writing a report about papyrus, or scarabs, or something. Why?'

'I think I've got her dad arrested.'

'Oh. That's not good.' They both loved Phuong's dad to distraction. 'How did you manage that?'

'He's being questioned about . . .' she lowered her voice still further, '*driving a white car around that night*. If you know what I mean.'

Estelle understood Veronique's cryptic message. 'Are you sure it's him?'

'It's a Vietnamese man.'

'There are quite a few of those in Paris.'

'OK – so maybe it isn't Phuong's dad. But if Phuong's stuck in the middle of Ancient Egypt, how can we find out if it's her dad?'

'You could ring him up.'

'Oh, that's a great idea,' snapped Veronique,

narrowing her eyes. 'And what am I supposed to say? *Hello – have you been arrested for killing Princess Diana?*'

'No. But you could say to whoever answers the phone, *Hello, it's Veronique here – do you have Phuong's address in Ancient Egypt?* and draw them into a general conversation that way. And if it's her dad who answers then you'll know straight away that he's not in jail.'

'Oh yes. That's actually quite a good idea, isn't it? Sorry I narrowed my eyes at you. As you can probably tell I'm in something of a frenzy.'

'For a change.'

'In fact I've got her parents' number in my book. I'll go and call them right now.'

'And will Madame be buying the dress?'

Veronique had forgotten all about it. She looked it up and down. 'No, I don't think so – it's a bit slutty for me.'

She found a public telephone, and dialled. Phuong's mother answered, and seemed in perfectly good spirits as she gave her Phuong's address in Cairo and told her all about their trip to see her. As she was running out of change, Veronique asked after Phuong's father. She was told he was very well – that he was upstairs painting the bathroom ceiling.

'And is he driving the same old car?' she asked.

'He can't drive,' said Phuong's mother. 'He doesn't know how, and yet he still has the audacity to call himself a man.'

'Of course,' said Veronique. 'I must have been thinking of somebody else. Say hello to him from me anyway.'

She felt elated as she started walking back to work, but this elation evaporated as she remembered that even if Phuong's dad was happily painting his bathroom ceiling, somebody she had never even met was having a miserable day thanks to her. She had finally had enough of it all.

She decided to get through the afternoon and go home to see César. She would change into some comfortable clothes and call the police to the house so they could see the half-dismantled Fiat, arrest her and let the poor man go. She was sick of the way she hadn't had the guts to face up to what she had done.

When she got back to the office, Françoise was delighted to see that she looked thoroughly miserable. Veronique moved the photo of her half-African niece and nephew so it pointed in Françoise's direction. Now, whenever she glared at her Françoise would be confronted with two prime examples of the dilution of her beloved French race, playing happily on a slide and looking so appealing it was almost unbelievable.

She said hello to César, had a shower, and changed into some comfortable questioning clothes – jeans, trainers, a T-shirt and a thick pullover in case they were to put her in a cold cell. She went downstairs and made herself a coffee. It was going to be a long night.

She turned on the radio to see if there was any news about the poor Vietnamese man. There was plenty. Not only had he had been released, he had also been completely ruled out of any kind of involvement in the crash. He had been at work at the time, and the ubiquitous panel of experts had declared that his car hadn't ever been in any kind of collision, let alone one in which a princess had died. The search was back on for the driver of the little white car.

Veronique hadn't much fancied spending the evening tied to a chair and being injected with truth serum, and was glad of the opportunity to just stay at home instead. The more she thought about it the less appealing the idea of confession, public vilification and a long, miserable imprisonment became. Jean-Pierre called, and she invited him to join her on her night off.

Even though she had wanted an evening without having to think too much about what had gone on, he insisted on watching a report about the latest developments in the investigation. They were using some fancy computer graphics to illustrate various people's ideas about what could have happened that night. A pair of witnesses had come forward to corroborate the evidence of the flakes of paint, saying they had seen a white Fiat Uno, driven by a worried-looking man, leaving the tunnel just after they heard the sound of the crash.

'What?' said Veronique. 'I'm not a man!'

'Get over it,' said Jean-Pierre. 'It'll make you look less suspicious.'

'I suppose so.' Veronique knew Françoise would be watching, and it would throw her off the scent. But even so.

'What?' she said, outraged again. 'César isn't a German Shepherd!'

'Again, I encourage you to think yourself lucky.'

'I suppose so. But a *German Shepherd*? I can understand them saying that there was a big dog in the back of the car – but why would they think he was a German Shepherd? I don't mind being misrepresented in the media, but César doesn't deserve it – he's done nothing wrong.'

'Not everybody is good at telling the difference between big dogs. Once more, you should be thankful.'

It was strange that hardly anyone had been around that night, and as the report went on it became apparent that nobody had really seen very much. The few stories that had emerged all seemed to contradict each other in one way or another, and there was even some implied speculation about the reliability of some of the witnesses, about how they could have been the kind of crazies who always appear around high-profile police investigations.

Jean-Pierre switched off the TV. 'I don't think any of that will affect Plan X too much.'

'Plan X? What's Plan X?'

'Er . . .' He had spoken without thinking. 'It's the name I thought up for what we're doing. Getting rid of the car and everything.' He looked embarrassed. 'Do you like it?'

'I love it!' She wished they had been calling it Plan X all along – it would have made it all so much more fun. 'But tell me honestly, do you think I look like a man?'

'Do you think I would be here if you did?'

'I was pretty drunk that night. Maybe the more I drink the more I start looking like a man.'

'You don't look like anything like a man, sober or not.'

'Well I'm definitely growing my hair back, just in case.'

'Never mind about all that. You'll be interested to hear about some progress I've made with Plan X.'

'What is it? Are you going to get me out of trouble once and for all?'

'I hope so. I've been making some enquiries, and I now know how to cut a car into lots of small pieces.'

'How did you manage that without giving the game away?'

'It was easier than I expected – I just developed a keen interest in post-industrial sculpture, and asked around in Bohemia. It turns out the first thing you learn at post-industrial sculpture school is how to cut up a car. There's no real mystery to it at all – an eight-year-old could do it, as long as they remember not to blow up the petrol tank. Anyway, I've arranged to borrow the equipment for a couple of days. I'll come round tomorrow and get started.'

'Jean-Pierre . . .' she almost said *I love you*, but she stopped herself just in time. 'Are you sure I don't look like a man?'

'You're insulting my girlfriend.'

'Sorry.'

He smiled. 'Just sit quietly and listen to this.' He had been sent an advance copy of one of the tracks he and his brother had written for the German band's album. It was called 'When We Made Love (I Thought It Would Last Forever)'. He was very pleased with the way it had turned out.

CHAPTER NINE

It hadn't taken much orchestration to get everyone together. Jean-Pierre didn't have a proper job, Estelle already had the day off, César was just a dog and would go along with more or less anything, and Veronique had called in sick. She didn't worry too much about being found out and getting the sack because she was planning on looking for a new job anyway – one that was less boring, that paid more and, more importantly, that didn't have Françoise sitting at the next desk. Every day since the release of the Vietnamese man Françoise had told her that she was seriously considering reporting her to the detectives in charge of the investigation so she could be *eliminated from their enquiries*, and every day she had thanked Françoise for her thoughtfulness but reminded her that since she wasn't a part of their enquiries to begin with, she didn't particularly need anybody's help to be eliminated from them.

It was with Françoise in mind that she had bought the car they were in. She had seen a Fiat Uno for sale near Jean-Pierre's apartment. It was three years younger than the one that had been sliced into pieces and bundled into the boot, and it was in better condition than the white one had been in the last time her parents had seen it. And, more importantly than all that, it was bright orange.

She hadn't realised that suburbia could be such a wonderful place. The street she lived on was lined with detached houses, none of them too big and none of them too small, all slightly different but somehow all the same, and each separated from the next by hedges, walls and fences. She had grown up deriding the neighbourhood for its apparent lack of life, but had recently come to learn that it was absolutely perfect when it came to nobody taking much notice of cars. The moment the mysterious

Fiat had been mentioned on the news she was sure that her neighbours would be straight on to the police about it, but nothing had happened. After all, its only distinguishing feature had been its mild decrepitude. Her parents were more or less retired, and preferred to spend their spare money on visiting their son and his family in Africa twice a year than on fancy cars, so they were unusual on their street for having an aged runaround as their only vehicle, but even so nobody seemed to pay this any attention, and besides it wasn't uncommon for wayward daughters such as Veronique to be presented with elderly and ordinary Fiats and Citroëns. Such resolutely anonymous cars drove up and down her road all the time.

When it first appeared in the street nobody had given it a second glance, when she drove it to the airport or to and from Jean-Pierre's nobody had paid the slightest attention, and when it suddenly disappeared from active service nobody had been any the wiser. It was hard to imagine a more perfect neighbourhood, or a more innocuous car.

They spent the morning driving around the city, discreetly taking an increasingly listless César for walks in many parks and dumping the bits in bins in as carefree a manner as they could muster. After lunch the bright orange Fiat disappeared into the garage to be re-loaded with plastic bags, then headed out into the countryside on its fourth and final trip of the day. Estelle was at the wheel, having insisted on driving, Veronique was in the back, almost smothered out of existence by a snoring Saint Bernard, and Jean-Pierre was in the passenger seat, still somewhat shell-shocked after two days in goggles and ear-muffs, having his bones shaken as he wrestled lumps of metal with a murderous circular saw. He hadn't even been able to open the garage door to let fresh air in, in case a gendarme happened to cycle past and take an interest, or the neighbours started to complain about the grating noise. It had been a horrible job.

They stopped in villages, in towns, and at any rest stops along the way where they could pretend they were stretching their legs, but where they were really dumping a bag or two in a litter bin. They left the very last bag in a small park in Étampes, and walked to a nearby bar to quietly celebrate.

Veronique and Jean-Pierre drank gin and tonic, and Estelle had an Orangina. 'Just so I don't accidentally kill a princess on the way home,' she explained.

It was dark by the time they got back to the house. Veronique got out to open the garage door, and from the corner of her eye she noticed somebody staring at her from a car across the street. Their seat was reclined, and they were clearly hoping they couldn't be seen, but as Estelle was parking the car Veronique walked over to see them. She leaned in through the open window.

'Hello Françoise,' she said.

'Er . . . hello.'

'And how are you?'

'I'm very well, thank you. And you?'

'I'm very well too. Fancy seeing you here.'

'Yes.'

'Goodnight,' said Veronique.

'Goodnight.'

Veronique walked back towards the house. When she was halfway across the street she heard Françoise calling her in a stage whisper.

'Françoise?' she said. 'You called?' She walked back towards the car.

'Veronique, I'm sorry.'

'What for?'

'You know what for – for spying on you. I just had to put my mind at rest.'

'Well, now you know.'

'Yes. But that wasn't you driving, was it? Why weren't you driving?'

'What difference does it make?'

'None really. But is it your car?'

'It's my bright orange Fiat, yes. The one I told you about.'

'Just out of interest,' she said, 'has it always been orange?' She was clutching at straws. She had done her research and was fairly sure the Fiat was too recent a model for it to have been the guilty car.

Veronique saw Françoise for what she really was. This was no great revelation, since she saw her for what she really was every day at work. 'Françoise?' she said.

'Yes?'

'Fuck you.' It felt good to say it, so she said it again. 'Fuck you, Françoise.'

'There's no need for that.'

'Yes there is.'

'Well, maybe there is a bit. But listen. Let's do a deal. If you don't tell anyone you caught me staking out your house, I won't tell anyone you weren't even slightly ill today. OK? I won't tell them you spent the day being driven around with your supposedly-ex-boyfriend and your dog.'

'OK.' Veronique had forgotten about her fake illness, and anyway her righteous indignation at having been spied on was beginning to ebb away. Françoise was, after all, completely correct to suspect that she had been involved in the crash, and she had come closer than the police ever had to catching her out. 'Let's just forget about it.'

Françoise put her seat back in position and started her car. Without another word, she drove away.

'So Jean-Pierre,' said Estelle, 'how are you finding your new calling as a post-industrial sculptor?'

He held up his hands, which were black with

oil and covered in scratches. 'To tell you the truth it's not going all that well. In fact I'm considering giving it up.'

'A promising talent wasted. It's such a shame.'

'Which reminds me,' he said. He went through to the garage and came back with three bits of twisted metal. He gave one each to Estelle and Veronique, and kept one for himself.

'Er,' said Veronique. 'What are these?'

'Can't you tell? They're souvenir ash trays made from the wreckage of the world famous car.'

'But what if the police find them?'

'They won't,' said Estelle. 'You've got away with it. Finally, Plan X is over. You don't have to worry about stuff like that any more. To the cops they would just be crappy old ash trays.'

'Hey,' said Jean-Pierre, 'I made them with great love and care.'

'Sorry. What I meant to say was that to the cops they would just be wonderful examples of utilitarian post-industrial sculpture.'

'That's better.' Jean-Pierre finished rolling an enormous joint. 'Hey, I've got an idea,' he said.

'Oh no,' said Veronique. 'What is it?'

'Let's listen to some music.'

'If we must.' She knew exactly what the music was going to be, but she didn't mind. After all, the money from it had saved her skin. She wondered whether all those German soft rock fans would still have bought the record if they had known how the songwriter's cut was going to be spent. All in, she owed Jean-Pierre somewhere around thirty thousand francs. He had told her she could pay him back whenever she was ready, but she was going to start as soon as she next got paid. She settled back in her chair and sang along to 'Like A Soldier (Of Shattered Dreams)'. When it finished she raised her glass and said, 'Happy birthday to me!'

Jean-Pierre and Estelle winced in unison.

'Ah,' said Estelle. 'Yes. Happy birthday.'

'Yes. Happy birthday,' said Jean-Pierre, clearing his throat and looking guilty.

'Don't worry,' said Veronique. 'You've done enough for me lately – I shouldn't expect you to remember my birthday as well as help me get rid of a car. Finishing Plan X is celebration enough. Listen, I am so grateful for everything you've done to get me out of this mess.'

'It's been fun,' said Estelle.

'Yes,' agreed a still guilty-looking Jean-Pierre. 'It's been great fun.'

Estelle excused herself, and Jean-Pierre grovelled quite horribly for having been so lax. The lights went out, and Estelle came back into the room carrying an enormous cake with twenty-three candles on it. She had made it herself, in the shape of a little white car.

Veronique was so touched that Estelle had not only remembered her birthday but had gone to all the trouble of making and hiding a cake that she burst into tears. 'At least I could rely on Jean-Pierre to forget my birthday,' she sobbed. 'If he had remembered as well, the emotion would probably have killed me.'

'Then maybe somebody should call an under-taker,' he said, as he reached into his bag and pulled out a card and a pair of parcels so small that they could only have contained some kind of jewellery.

*   *   *

Full of cake and wine, and slumped in her seat with her hand on her belly, Veronique was lost in thought. Plan X may have been over for Estelle and Jean-Pierre, but she still had one more river to cross. In less than twenty-four hours' time her parents would be back, and wondering why their car had turned orange in their absence.

CHAPTER TEN

Veronique noticed that her mother and father looked particularly tanned as they wheeled their trolley into the arrivals hall at Charles de Gaulle airport. 'You look brown,' she said.

She was taken aback by how pleased they were to see her. They threw their arms around her and kissed her over and over again. She had to keep reminding herself that they had no idea what she had been up to while they had been away. As far as they knew she had been a model daughter, working hard and doing a good job of looking after their house. They had no idea she had been having sex with strangers, stealing high-class audio equipment and killing princesses.

Walking up ramps and waiting for elevators, her parents talked about Benin, and about the children, and when they reached the car they were delighted to see she had brought César along to meet them. They fussed around him for a while, and got in. Veronique drove away.

It wasn't until they were almost home that her mother noticed something. 'I thought this car was white,' she said.

'I was wondering about that too,' said her father. 'But I didn't like to say anything.'

'Veronique?'

'Yes, mother?'

'Why is the car suddenly orange?'

'Oh,' said Veronique, her excuse prepared to the last syllable, 'I'd forgotten all about that. It's a long story.'

'Will you tell us?'

'OK, when we get home. You must be dying for a coffee.'

She was right. They were both dying for a coffee.

'Well,' explained Veronique, 'the day after you left, the clutch went on the white car. I could hardly drive it at all, and it was making terrible noises every time I changed gear. So I found the number of the dealer from Normandy who sold it to you and I called him and gave him a piece of my mind – I asked him how he had the cheek to sell a car with a bad clutch.'

'And what did he say?' asked her mother.

'Nothing at first – he just burst into tears.'

'The poor man.'

'He was devastated. When he pulled himself together he explained that he had never sold a bad car before, and that he would be round the very next day with a replacement – one which was much better in every way, except that it was bright orange.'

'It is certainly very orange.'

'Yes,' agreed her father. 'One of the main things about it is that it's very orange indeed.'

'Anyway, the next morning he arrived here in the orange car. He cursed the white one, and kicked it, and took it to be fixed at a place around the corner, and then he drove back to Normandy in it.'

'That was nice of him.'

'Yes, he was full of apologies.'

'But there was no need for him to have taken

it quite so badly. I mean, it's a car, and cars go wrong all the time. It was pretty old too, and we knew it was a risk when we bought it. To tell you the truth I think we would have been surprised if he had even offered to pay for a new clutch.'

'But it was the first complaint he had ever had in nearly thirty years of selling cars, and he was falling over himself to replace it with a better model. You can tell just by looking at it that it's worth more than the other one.'

'Well,' said her mother, turning to her father, 'we should go and see him next time we're up there, and thank him for being so fair.'

'Yes, we must. We should take him a gift.'

'No,' said Veronique. 'You mustn't.'

'Why ever not?' asked her mother.

She hadn't rehearsed this far. She had simply assumed that her parents would accept her meticulously thought-out explanation, drop the subject and start showing her photos. Still, she had become quite accomplished at thinking on her feet. 'Because,' she said, 'he wouldn't want you to.'

'But why on earth wouldn't he want us to say

thank you and give him a lovely pot of honey, or an imitation Beninese bronze?'

'He said he didn't want that.'

'What? Did he tell you *specifically* that he didn't want any bee products or reproduction west-African ornaments? Maybe we could think of something else to give him.'

'No, he doesn't want anything at all.'

'Really? What a strange man.'

'He was so upset about it all that he asked me never to mention it again. He understood that I would have to explain the new car to you two, but he fell to his knees and begged me never to tell anybody else about the clutch trouble, and particularly never to say a word about it to him again. I assured him it was a closed book, that it would never, *ever* be spoken of again by any of us. He even made me promise that we wouldn't raise the subject after his death. He told me he wouldn't be able to find peace in his final moments if he thought the clutch business was going to be dragged up after he was gone.'

'For a used car salesman he seems to have reacted quite unusually to being caught selling a dodgy old

Fiat,' said her father. 'But who are we to complain? You know, I've always quite fancied having a bright orange car, and now I've got one. If you look at it like that it's almost like a dream come true.'

'What? You never told me you dreamed of driving an orange car,' said Veronique's mother. She looked at her daughter. 'You live with somebody for thirty-two years – you wash their socks, you bear their children, and you think you know them inside out and then they spring something like that on you. *Orange cars* indeed – if I had known you were so easily pleased I would have made a lot less effort over the years.'

'Maybe that's why I never mentioned it,' he said. 'Anyway, he can consider the matter closed. I will never even think of it again.'

They stayed up late. Veronique admired her imitation Beninese bronzes, which she would add to the extensive collection that had been somewhat forced upon her over the last three or four years, and none of them could stop looking at the photos of the extraordinary children her brother had somehow managed to produce.

PART THREE

CHAPTER ONE

Sometimes Veronique wished the princess would come to her in a dream. She wanted her to appear in the middle of the night, to take her by the hand and tell her not to worry about what she'd done. She wanted to hear mild platitudes, like *some things are meant to be*, and *there's no point in being dragged down by your mistakes – it's best just to learn from them and move on.*

She had a dream in which she was wearing a watch that was also a fish tank, another where she was trapped inside a panda costume, and in another she was suckling a really odd-looking baby. But the princess never came to stroke her hair and tell her not to worry.

*   *   *

For months newspapers and magazines had been full of all kinds of speculation about what had happened that night. Some people had concluded that MI6 and the CIA must have come together and executed Diana and her Egyptian lover to ensure that the future king of England wouldn't end up with a Muslim for a stepfather. Others blamed agents employed by major players in the international arms trade, who had been disgruntled with her for pointing out to the world that the land mines they produced often tore innocent people to shreds, and there were rumours of private armies, lone assassins and jealous lovers.

She was always interested to hear versions of events that placed her centre stage. In one of them she, or maybe her canine sidekick, had been deliberately dazzling the other car's driver by shining a blinding light in his eyes, and in another she and César had taken over the steering of the doomed Mercedes with an elaborate remote-control device. In both scenarios her parents' second hand Fiat had been secretly armour-plated and fitted with a turbo-charged engine so it could get away from the scene at lightning speed.

She understood why so many people were ready to listen to all these theories, no matter how far-fetched they were. A suicide pact with her lover would have had more romance, a powerboat flipping over in the Seychelles more drama; a private jet vanishing in the Bermuda Triangle would have had more mystery, or a slow descent into seclusion and alcoholism more poignancy. Even a re-creation of Isadora Duncan's scarf trick, or of Grace Kelly's plunge from a mountain pass would have been somehow more satisfying than a collision with a concrete pillar. To the people weeping in the streets almost anything would have been preferable to her meeting her end in an ugly underpass, even if it was in the heart of the City of Love, and even if they did find strings of pearls and a solid gold cigar clipper among the wreckage.

Amid the wild speculation came the occasional fact about the crash, and as each one emerged Veronique shook a little more responsibility from her shoulders. She found out that the driver of the other car had drunk four times more than he should have done, had been going at twice the speed limit, and had jumped red lights in a car he wasn't even qualified to drive. She also heard that none of the people who died had been using a seatbelt during their high-speed car chase, as if they thought they were invincible, and she could hardly take the blame for that.

Sometimes the Fiat would be mentioned in passing on the news. At one point it was announced that the owners of all such cars in Paris were obliged to present themselves to the police. She responded to this instruction by pretending she hadn't heard it. Her parents' car had been registered in Normandy, and as far as she knew there had never been any record of it having been in Paris. Anyway, by this time there was something suspiciously perfunctory about the whole investigation. The police gave the impression that they would much rather have been out catching criminals than looking for a car that may or may not have played a minor role in a straight-forward drink-driving accident some time before.

But no matter what was revealed by the detectives and the press in the months following the crash, one crucial factor was never mentioned – that a girl who had just left her boyfriend had been driving around with a bellyful of wine and a joint in her hand, listening to the radio and talking to her dog. And if she hadn't been, then the princess would probably have made it safely to wherever it was she was going.

CHAPTER TWO

Jean-Pierre had seen it as a sign.

With Plan X behind them at last, he and Veronique had made a series of calls to a suspicious Clément. He had been somewhat reluctant to help them out but eventually, to get rid of them, he told them the name of the dealer he had sold the stereo to. They raced over to his shop in the bright orange car, and Jean-Pierre jumped out while it was still moving. By the time Veronique had parked and caught up with him he had found his amplifier, his speakers, his tuner and his CD player. The tape deck had already been sold, but he was happy enough with what he had found. After a brief explanation of the equipment's provenance, he managed to negotiate a tiny discount, and loaded his stereo into the boot.

Back at his apartment he sorted out the leads and switched it on. There was a warm pop from the speakers, and the CD tray glided out. And there before him, shining like an angel, sat *Where Soundwaves Turn To Sound* by The Sofia Experimental Breadboard Octet.

He visited a few potential venues, and spoke to some people who could sort out the lights and sound. He made a list of everything he would need and what it would all cost, and worked out how much money he could afford to risk. And when he had done all that he wrote a long letter to Bulgaria. He hoped he had found a path to atonement for his crimes against music – in bringing The Sofia Experimental Breadboard Octet to Paris he would begin to make amends for the pollution he had brought to the airwaves with songs like '(You Are) So Attractive (To Me)', and 'I've Never Loved A Lady (Like You)'. It was going to be a long, long journey, but he was taking his first faltering steps in the right direction.

Veronique hadn't tacitly announced their separation by sitting at the Taj Mahal as a rat scurried symbolically at her feet, and no castle had been engulfed in flames to mark their parting. Things had been flat between them for a while – they had both felt it wasn't going anywhere but neither of them could ever quite get around to ending it. While they were in Madrid for Veronique's exhibition they had been lying silently on opposite sides of their hotel bed, not having nearly as much fun as they should have been as they half-watched home video footage of hapless villagers being trampled by bulls on Impacto TV. She said to him, *This isn't really working, is it?* and he replied *No, not really,* and they went out and got drunk on gin and tonic.

When they got back in at dawn Jean-Pierre fell asleep on the floor, and that was that.

She hadn't left her job after all. She and Marie-France still had their desk next to Françoise (whose dress sense had continued to deteriorate (one day she had even come to work wearing a bonnet), and she had taken on three nights a week waiting on tables in the restaurant of a fancy hotel to help dig herself out of the financial hole she was in. She kept paying Jean-Pierre his two thousand francs a month, and after a couple of weeks of giving each other a wide berth things were fine between them. He found himself an eighteen-year-old girlfriend, who hung on his every word and never doubted that he made his living by just writing occasional film and music reviews and playing his gigantic saxophone as part of a quartet in half-empty bars twice a week. He didn't feel the need to tell her about his ongoing achievements in the field of power balladry. He and his brother had had nine songs recorded, with varying degrees of commercial success. The cheques were coming in quite steadily, and that was how he was able to afford to move into his big apartment on the Left Bank. Veronique went to visit him every once in a while, and once she teased him about how he was finally living the dream he had gone on about for so long.

'Of course I could never have moved from my old apartment before, no matter how much I wanted to,' he said.

'Yes you could – you could have moved here and pretended to be Argentinian any time if you had just made the effort. It used to make me mad.'

'But you don't understand.'

'What don't I understand? That it's hard to get around to moving house when you're stoned all the time?'

'No. I couldn't have moved, no matter how much I wanted to, because if I had left that apartment my parents would probably have sold it.'

'So?'

'So what about Uncle Thierry? Can you imagine telling him that he couldn't go to that window and set his pigeons flying any more? Could you have done that to him?'

She felt a wave of love hit her, but she didn't do anything about it. She was confident that if she just ignored it, it would turn fuzzy and go away. That was what usually happened.

*　　*　　*

Estelle couldn't work out why on earth Veronique's doctor had invited her and Phuong to the wedding when he had only met them a few times. Veronique explained that his bride was going to have four ex-boyfriends in the congregation, and since he only had one ex-girlfriend to invite he was going to feel somewhat outnumbered. Three mysterious French girls turning up on his side of the church would make him seem like slightly less of a hopeless case. Estelle had been reluctant to travel all the way to England so that somebody she barely knew could pretend that he had once been an international ladies' man, and when Veronique announced that she couldn't go because her brother would be over with his babies that weekend, and Phuong said she was going to be away logging the movements of jellyfish off the coast of Chile, she struck the whole thing out of her diary. That was until she discovered that in fact the bride wasn't English at all, but Welsh, and the wedding was going to be taking place on the Llyn peninsula, the home of her beloved R.S. Thomas. She wrote back straight away, accepting the invitation.

*   *   *

She had caused some confusion on the day. Nobody could quite work out where she had come from, or what she was doing there on her own. She spent most of her time charging around the bride's relatives, frantically practising her Welsh and asking them if they had any R.S. Thomas stories to tell. The sight of a blonde French girl in six-inch heels and a very small zebra print dress had stirred up quite a commotion. Men queued up to practise their Welsh with her, as their wives and girlfriends looked on from the corners of their eyes. She was very impressed with the doctor's choice of bride, and sobbed out loud as they exchanged their vows. At the reception she found herself in conversation with the church organist. He was a softly-spoken man of thirty-nine who lived with his mother and had an extensive knowledge of his country's poetic and hymnal traditions in both the Welsh and English languages. Halfway through his dissection of the ending of Dylan Thomas's story 'A Visit To Grandpa's', which she hadn't read, she silenced him with a long and passionate kiss. He had been quite taken aback, because it was the first time anyone had ever kissed him and he had long since given up hoping.

She made him take her home. They crept quietly up the stairs and into his room, and before long bedsprings were creaking and low moans were echoing around the house. A knock came at the door of the room, and then another, then the knocking became pounding and his mother shouted: 'You stop that right this minute. It's disgusting.'

'I'm sorry mother,' the organist called back, 'but it may be the only chance I ever get.' He went back to his task with renewed vigour, and eventually the banging on the door and the shouting stopped.

In the morning his mother was waiting at the breakfast table for her son and his brazen new friend. She was startled by the sight of the French girl in her very short, low cut and impossibly tight dress, and even more startled by the free and easy conversation she made in perfectly passable Welsh over her boiled egg. She showed an interest in the house and the village, and by the time she had finished her second cup of tea the organist's mother found herself quite delighted by her, and she said, 'You must come back and see us again one day. That would be nice, wouldn't it Rhodri?'

Rhodri looked at his shoes.

'I'm afraid that won't be possible,' Estelle explained on his behalf.

'I already invited her,' said Rhodri quietly, still looking at his shoes, 'and she already said no. She tells me it's for the best, and that I should trust her because she knows about that kind of thing.'

Estelle stepped into her preposterous shoes, said her goodbyes and left the house. She went back to her B&B, changed into some slightly more appropriate clothes and took a taxi to Aberdaron, where she sat in the rear pew of a small church and was transfixed by the back view of a grumpy-looking old man. He didn't get up to say anything, he just carried on like any other member of the congregation, and at the end of the service she stayed where she was and he walked right past her on his way out, so close she could smell him, and he smelled perfect – exactly the way she had imagined he would, of words and of Wales. She didn't ask for his autograph, and she didn't even say hello. She just followed him outside and watched him until he was out of sight. And then, walking on air, she took the taxi to the railway station and headed back to London. She had something left to do before going back to France.

'She seemed very nice after all that,' said the organist's mother.

'I know,' he said.

'She was very pretty, wasn't she? And she knew all sorts of things about Wales. And I suppose what she did to you last night is just normal behaviour in France so we shouldn't hold it against her all that much, should we? Maybe it's time you started looking out for a lovely girl like that. Now are you sure she won't come back to see you?'

Rhodri said nothing.

'Rhodri?'

He didn't reply.

'Rhodri, I'm talking to you.'

'She's never coming back, mother. Please let's never mention her again.' He carried on looking at his shoes. He couldn't imagine a moment when he would ever take his eyes off them, not if he lived to be a hundred. He didn't know why, but he kept seeing visions of a walled vegetable garden and a bloodhound, and he felt in his heart the beginnings of a longing that would never go away.

CHAPTER THREE

Jean-Pierre hadn't realised that the night he had chosen for his concert was exactly a year after Veronique's fateful drive home. She hadn't realised it either, until she had turned on the television that morning and seen a mawkish *one-year-on* feature on the news, but there was too much going on for either of them to give it much thought. The preparations had gone slowly but very well – all four hundred tickets had sold out in advance, and at the last minute Jean-Pierre had discreetly arranged to squeeze another fifty people into the impossibly trendy art gallery he had chosen as a venue. On hearing this Veronique, who had been recruited to help out on the day, decided to do a timely good deed by trying to get him to donate all the profit from the concert to an anti-land-mine organisation.

'OK,' he said, casually. 'If you want.'

'That's great – how much do you think it'll raise?'

'Well, let me think . . .' He had been a long way out with his predictions, and when all the hidden costs of arranging a concert by fourteen Bulgarians were taken into account, even with the extra fifty tickets he was in line to make quite a significant loss. 'About minus fifteen thousand francs. If you could ask your charity to send me a cheque as soon as possible I would be very grateful.'

'Ah,' said Veronique.

'It's not that big a deal,' he said, shrugging his shoulders. 'Such is the nature of redemption.'

She spent the rest of the day filling baguettes for Bulgarians, and realising where all the money had gone. She'd had no idea avant-garde musicians had such appetites.

Veronique cursed Jean-Pierre for having sneaked those fifty extra people in. By ten thirty the room was packed, and it was going to be a nightmare moving around and fulfilling her role as the official photographer. Estelle appeared, having pushed through the crowd taking care that nobody stepped on her left foot. She was wearing a pair of Brigitte's big trainers, and limping. 'How's your toe?' asked Veronique, embracing her.

'It's OK – it'll hurt for a while, but they told me it'll be completely stuck back on before long. You should have done it too – you'd have been able to pay Jean-Pierre back in one go, and have money left over to lavish on your new boyfriend.'

'I don't have a new boyfriend any more.' After ten and a half months of agony the man from the garage had finally found the courage to go back to her house and ask her out. Even though she had been going out of her way to stay single he had seemed pretty low-maintenance so she thought she might as well give him another try. She hadn't bargained on his romantic streak though, and after two weeks she decided to put an end to it all. 'I ran out of vases,' she explained. 'And poor César was getting fat on all the treats he kept bringing round.

When I sent him away he told me he was going to join the army, but I don't know if he did. Anyway, never mind me – how was Wales?'

Estelle's eyes misted over. 'It was perfect.'

'And my doctor?'

'He was very well.'

'And what about his wife? What's she like?'

'I'm afraid she's very nice.'

'But a bit funny-looking, I suppose?'

'No, not really. In fact she's quite beautiful. I'm sorry about that.'

'She's probably not all that bright, then.'

The house lights went down, and a reverent hush descended on the audience. A man walked on to the makeshift stage and reached inside an open baby grand piano. He gently tapped one of its strings, over and over again. Then a woman walked on, sat down and put the ends of two wires together, causing a strange-looking machine to make a humming sound. Then she walked on again, only it wasn't her – it was her identical twin, who picked up a ukulele and started to play it upside-down. One by one they arrived, until all fourteen members of

The Sofia Experimental Breadboard Octet were on stage, doing what they do best.

After the third encore the lights went up and the audience reluctantly started heading towards the door. Jean-Pierre wandered by, apparently lost in a state of ecstasy. Veronique took a photo of him. The flash snapped him out of his reverie and he walked over to her. 'That was great,' she said. 'Everyone loved it.'

'I know.' She had never seen him so happy, and couldn't help giving him a hug. Within seconds his girlfriend had glided silently to his side, and she had to let him go. 'We're going back to my place now,' he said. He was hosting a party for the band and a few carefully selected guests to celebrate the Bulgarians having created a soundscape in Paris. 'Are you coming with us?'

'I'll follow on,' she said.

He left the gallery, his arm around his girlfriend's shoulders. Veronique was surprised he had gone for somebody so tall. She looked at her watch. It was 12:25. She waited. It turned 12:26, exactly one year from her drive through the tunnel. She watched each second pass. The minute went by unremarkably, with no apparitions, no earthquake, no spectral voices and no bolt of lightning. She felt a knot in her stomach, but that was all. At 12:27 she packed her camera away, yawned and found Estelle among the stragglers. They headed off to Jean-Pierre's. It was going to be a long night. The octet had requested more baguettes.